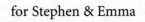
for Stephen & Emma

Unable to find peace within myself, I made use of the external surroundings to calm my spirit, and unable to find delight within my heart, I borrowed a land-scape to please it. Therefore, strange were my travels.

—T'u Lung

1

NEW YORK CITY, 1993

Down at the Fulton Fish Market, a person could still buy the illegal eels pulled from the Hudson, eels that had evolved, in the last one or two hundred generations, an enzyme that resists the PCBs and that is, according to people who have a bent for this sort of thing, very tasty, laces the meat with a flavor that is, as Peter described it, woody and vibrant. It's the eel's response to the modern world, to General Electric in particular, and Peter believed he could taste this. Though Peter believed he could taste anything in an animal: age, history, strength, fear. You could say he was an antivegetarian— loved bodies, claws, forms, hooves, ribs, though I guess his favorite food was still the litchi nuts he picked up every morning on his way in to work, as he passed through Chinatown. He lived in Cobble Hill, in Brooklyn, took the F to East Broadway, and then walked up through Chinatown to our office on Houston Street.

Peter and I ran a nonprofit called the Aquinas Foundation. Actually, Peter was its founder, and I worked for him. Officially the mission of Aquinas was to promote the intersection of Eastern and Western medicine. Unofficially, Aquinas was the practical arm of Peter's fancy. Our most visible project and our most troubling was something Peter called a "healing center," which was to be built on the edge of the Yangtze River in China. It helped to think of it as not quite hospital, not quite spa, not quite temple, but a mixture of all three, some organization of materials devoted to fulfilling a person's mental and physical potential. At first I had thought the project would be a very difficult sell, donorwise, but instead it had appealed deeply to that strange human bird, the celebrity, many of whom felt such a place was utterly legitimate, since they themselves required close, intricate types of attention—acupuncture, biofeedback, qi gong—but were not actually sick in any way. Money was rolling in from them.

This morning I was again battling over the phone with a man we called the Gripper. Peter and I stood side by side looking out at Soho, both of us with headsets on. The Gripper was a Hollywood agent and lawyer, and he was very stealthy and demanding. Once at a party I had seen him eat an olive and then split the pit with his teeth, sucking out some private and nasty goodness within.

Today he was insisting that his client's name be on the

center, on a plaque. "I want his name on the hospital itself," the Gripper said.

"It's not a hospital," I said. "It's a healing center."

"Whatever it is. I don't care. He needs more recognition."

"That's what he *needs*?" I said, trying to emphasize the word *need* in order to suggest how ironic it was in this context. And anyway, this plaque was going to be on a building that was nearly toppling into the Yangtze River, not exactly a high-traffic area.

"Listen," the Gripper said. "Do you think my client needs for his career your little Noodle House?"

Peter smiled wanly at this. We'd been trying to dream up a name for our project, something that would pay allegiance to its mysteries and healing powers, something vaguely Asian, but from that moment on, almost against our will, we called it only the Noodle House.

And then I noticed Peter's hands were trembling a little, which meant the conversation had to end, since he needed insulin or juice or crackers, or maybe just rest. I could never guess exactly what he needed at any moment, given his diabetes. Somehow he calibrated and controlled it all—the rise and fall of his sugar and insulin levels, the tiny waves in his blood—by a very careful monitoring of sleep and food and emotions. Sometimes I thought this was what was responsible for his extraordinary appeal and attraction, the fact that he was keeping his body together by dint of his own will alone.

"We'll figure out something by tomorrow," I said.

"That's fine," he said. "We'll figure it out." He was preparing his little needle. "Good job, little one," he said to me.

So I'm thirty-one, and not really anybody's idea of little, but Peter first knew me twenty years ago, when I was ten and he was twenty-eight. Peter was then working for Richard Nixon, one of those young Democrats Nixon was said to love to hire and to keep under his thumb. Peter was doing some combination of diplomacy and intelligence, first in Cambodia and then in Beijing, during the time my family was also living in Beijing, my parents both Christian missionaries. Peter came to our little house on Fuling Street frequently, and eventually fell in love with my beloved amah, Su Chen. I recall him standing in our small kitchen, trying to help Su Chen cook, hovering over her as she scooped squid parts out of the soup or tied up the wings of little game hens. When she wasn't taking care of me, Su Chen was earning her Ph.D. at Beijing Normal, and like many students, she was a Red Guard. She was alive with optimism for Mao, and many afternoons we would make poster boards at our kitchen table for one struggle session or another—*Defeat the Running Dogs! Advance wave upon wave!*

By 1973, after Mao's dream had curdled, almost all foreigners, including my family and Peter, had begun to flee the country. My family moved back to New York City, where my parents had long ago met and married, and Peter went away on a boat, toward I never knew where at the time, just into distance, where his people were. But Su Chen never left at all—she went first to Zhongnanhai, and then to a labor camp near Mongolia, and then even farther north, which is death. Her soul, according to Mao and Marx before him, would have stayed woven to her body, as the brightest thread is still part of the fabric, still there, under her snowy grave west of Chang-Chun-Sa.

2

By the time Peter's second insulin shot of the day rolled around, about 4:30 in the afternoon, I was getting ready to go, glancing through the last of the day's mail. There were mostly just bills and one disturbing notice from the IRS, asking me once again to outline just how it was our organization fell within the guidelines of a charity for tax purposes. I had to explain this every year, and each time I tried to sound more and more certain of our status, though my confidence was dissipating with each explanation. I put the letter under some other papers that I didn't want to deal with at the moment, in what was essentially my denial pile. And then there was a personal letter just for me. It had my name on it. I recognized the handwriting immediately—precise, well-mannered, cursive.

Dear Justine:
Last time we spoke it went so poorly that it seemed ten years of silence was the only appropriate response. The

details are lost now, but I'm sure I was pressuring you unduly. Where are you? I've heard that you are in Manhattan, right under my nose? I'm here, of course, still a traitor. I'd like to see you.

James Nutter. Nutter-Butter. The last I'd heard he'd written a screenplay that had sold to one of the movie studios in Hollywood, about a girl superhero, of all things. James and I had been young together, in our early twenties, though even then he had seemed much older, like a gentleman farmer or something, dropped into the chaos of a college dorm. He lived a floor above me, and we spent nearly every second together, often walking around late at night. We were like an old married couple in that way, crisscrossing Harvard Yard, past the plain, pilgrim-y beauty of the Unitarian church, through its sad city graves, down Appian Way, skirting Radcliffe Yard, and into the residential streets of Cambridge—the seemingly ramshackle but actually beautifully kept houses along narrow winding roads, under branches of cherry trees that rose—incandescent, fleeting—into the night sky. It reminded me of childhood somehow, though not my own; I'd grown up on the seventeenth floor of a building along Central Park West. As for James, he'd grown up in Saskatchewan, in the most classic childhood of all, the one that is burning away in all of us—a small and simple farmhouse set deep in a grove of trees, surrounded by concentric, golden fields of wheat.

"What's up?" Peter said as I read the letter. "Who's it from?"

"Nobody," I said. "Just somebody I used to know."

Peter leaned back in his chair and tilted his head back, his silvery and feathered hair curling at the neckline, as he let the insulin—balmy, healing—work its way into his bloodstream. He could look a little debauched in this pose. "That's the saddest thing I ever heard," he said. "Somebody you used to know."

3

The rain battered against the windows with such force, and at such a strange, windswept angle, that it felt like the city itself was casting water up against our office. I was there early, in order to intercept whatever faxes might come in from China and then interpret them for Peter. He needed, I thought, to be protected from the day-to-day floundering of our project there. The left hand, as it says early in the book of Matthew, need not always know what the right hand does. I did tell him what I thought he absolutely needed to know, but only in the proper time, sometimes long after the crisis had passed.

Sure enough, this morning there was bad news from the Yangtze. Yiang-Yang, who was our liaison in Beijing, called me as soon as I arrived. It was late at night in China. "Justine," she said, in her low, tonal Mandarin accent, "I have heard that the Three Gorges Dam might be extended."

"Does Peter know?" I asked.

"Not yet."

"What have you heard?"

"Just a rumor that they're voting tomorrow on an extension. In a moment I'll be faxing you a map of the proposed changes. It doesn't look good."

"Okay. I'll call you back."

"I see you," she said. And then came the fax, along whose shiny paper ran the Yangtze in its meandering way. Even on paper, in representation, it was a beautiful river, sliding and bending across nine provinces, skirting Tibet, plummeting through China and then ending at the sea. And where the Noodle House was to be, on a jagged cliff overlooking a bend in the river at Shanxi Province, there was a circle drawn and filled in by Yiang-Yang with little calligraphic waves, meaning it would be gone if the dam extension were to pass. Lately Yiang-Yang had been doing this a lot, sending me faxes with desperate little diagrams of how bad the situation was getting. I think she must have been worried that we didn't quite understand how doomed this project might be.

And then came Peter, in his regulation white shirt and khakis, as well as a long raincoat. As was usually the case, I told him about the fax, soft-pedaling the contents, but he never laid eyes on it himself. He could worry overly. He could think too hard for us, which is maybe the art of charity. I said that there was a rumor circulating that the dam's dimensions might be increasing, but it looked very doubtful.

I did feel around a bit, making my way blindly through his dreams, which was sort of the definition of my job. "And if the extension goes through, what then?"

"It's unimaginable," he said.

"True," I said. "But really, what would make you cancel this project?"

"I would have to be a different person entirely," he said. "And you?"

"Me?"

"Where is the line beyond which you wouldn't step?"

My feelings for Peter had sailed me so far over that line that I hadn't even noticed its passing, long ago. On the day we met, when I was still a child, Peter had picked me up at my school in Beijing, a private school dotted with foreigners. He had lifted me into the air and onto his shoulder. "You are Justine," he'd said to me, shouting over the winds. A thunderstorm was threatening. My classmates and I had been out in the unusually heightened air playing a game of airplane, which was a pose people had to take in those days for various thought crimes. You'd see them standing precariously in the backs of moving rickshaws, one leg kicked out at the back and the arms extended, an excruciating position to maintain for any length of time.

"What were you chanting?" Peter shouted to me after he'd scooped me up and was carrying me through the enormous gusts of wind and rain, toward the little path that would take us through a small grove of trees, down past Asia Food Store, and to Fuling Street. From Fuling Street you could see down a nearly sheer cliff to a little inlet. On this day, huge pieces of litter—Styrofoam—were rolling into shore, and they looked beautiful and spooky, nearly fluorescent in the darkening water. My face was buried deeply in the cove of Peter's neck.

"*The sun in my heart is Mao Tse-tung!*" I lifted my face to sing to him. It was a poem every child sang in school.

"The sun in your heart is Mao Tse-tung?"

"*The sun in my heart is Mao Tse-tung. Won't the goddess of the hills be surprised when she sees what Mao has done?*" I sang it into his ear. I pushed back his wet hair so he could hear me over the wind. His hair was sandy blond, and his skin was a little pitted. He was sweating, exuberant. I knew that Su Chen loved him.

"Ah," he said. "The goddess of the hills! She'll be surprised."

Back in our little house, when Peter and I came in, soaking wet, Su Chen bent down to kiss me. She was rolling two-inch squares of sticky rice around pork and seaweed. Her face was stern and friendly and concerned. Su Chen was writing her dissertation on the political themes in the *The Story of the Stone,* China's most famous novel, written in the mid-1700s, and she supported herself by working for my family. Just by thinking of Su Chen's face now, I can perceive all of her lessons for me, which essentially could all be resolved into the lesson of *jiangling*, which means to be beautiful on the inside but plain on the outside. Su Chen believed this was the definition of "right womanhood," as she called it. Su Chen was of the first generation of women in her family who didn't bind their feet, who didn't teeter like lilies at a pond's edge. She was a student and a revolutionary—flat-footed, practical, hardworking. Su Chen would just look at me, and I would see *jiangling* in her eyes. "Justine," she would say, "you are a standard-bearer. *Jiangling!*"

So now, another rainy day, twenty years later, and back in New York City, Peter's question reverberated in my mind for a few seconds, a ridiculous question really, given our history. Where was the line beyond which I would not step?

"I can't begin to answer that," I said.

He slid into his chair and started his morning ritual, which was not quite self-destructive, more like self-provocative. He opened his bag of litchi nuts, still on their stems. They had rugged little jackets, a coconut brown with a similar rough down. Inside they were basically sugar and water, in the flesh of a large, white, peeled grape. He didn't eat that many of them usually, just enough to send his blood sugar soaring and require his first midmorning hit of insulin. I maintained always that he shouldn't eat the litchi nuts, but I could see that they might be helping him to order his day around vigilance and thoughtfulness. And though it may have been harder in the long run on his system, perhaps his eating fructose first thing in the day was a sort of spiritual resistance to his diabetes, that complex vine planted in his blood.

Nothing more was said that day about the dam, which amounted to a subtle lie on my part. That day may have been the start of our troubles, since later in the afternoon, after I'd left the office to go to a show at the Whitney with my friend Bonnie-Beth, Peter had returned from the class he taught at the New School, promptly called Yiang-Yang, and set in motion a stage of our plan from which there was no turning back. Yiang-Yang herself must have been surprised that, only a few hours after receiving potentially devastating news, the two Americans had decided to launch full-scale into their fever dream, instructing her to hire over two hundred more workers, thereby tying up a few more hundred fates with the Noodle House, this mercurial, unstable, not-to-really-be-believed East-West dream of peace and rest profound.

4

The Three Gorges Dam was dreamt up by Sun Yat-sen in the early 1900s as a message to the rest of the world that China was a superpower, the dragon of the East, and not even nature stood in its way. The dream survived the whole tumultuous century, winding down through the Nationalists to the Communists, outlasting the Cultural Revolution, the Great Leap Forward, Mao's death, the trial of Madame Mao, and now even the Tiananmen massacre.

When the great dragon, as Mao described the dam, at last enters China, beginning in the year 2001 and completed in the year 2008, it will knock out a thousand villages, 9 million statues of the Buddha, and 172 species of wildlife, including the snow leopard, who has been a companion to the Yangtze for two thousand years, sipping from its wild banks. Also, the giant China sturgeon will have disappeared, the most ancient fish in the world, who in pictures looks so tired and blasé, his having seen the whole world unfold from there under the waves.

The dam will also affect many pharmaceutical companies worldwide, since along its banks grow fields of poppies. In the wet season these flowers blow around, or actually seem to jump a little in their places, happy and demented. Eventually the wind separates the blooms from their bodies, and the seedpods—dry, gravid, perfectly round, almost impossibly heavy atop such slender stalks—come in. At the precise moment before the seedpod is about to topple over of its own weight, it is harvested for its opium, a black, molasses-type substance, which oozes out when the pod is touched even with a pinprick and from which of course comes the glorious profusion—morphine, heroin, codeine, Demerol—all those effortless ways off the express train. There are plenty of places to grow poppies, of course, especially across Asia, but it did seem a little sad that those particular fields, their fragile poppy heads shaking in the breezes off the Yangtze, were soon to be drowned. I guess my sadness about this all was a bit selfish, since in my deepest fantasies, there was a room in the Noodle House with my name on it, where I could retreat from the world and become whole again, staring out at the bloodred fields, and at the Yangtze floating away alongside, serene and fast, wild and peaceful, blue-black at twilight.

5

I was surprised by how easy it was to get James's phone number through directory assistance, and then to get his voice on the machine. "James," I said, "I got your note. Also, I ran into Clover, who lives up in Midtown. He said you'd sold your script. Congratulations! He also asked if we were married. It seems we're not. Call me!"

6

The next afternoon Peter was at the library doing some prep work for the urban design seminar he taught when I received a visit from our landlord and intermittent benefactor, the debonair but vaguely insane Mr. John Burns. Mr. Burns, like myself, was enamored of Peter, yet Peter couldn't bear to spend five minutes with him, so it was left to me to sustain Mr. Burns's interest in Aquinas. I actually found him endearing in some ways; he had a rich, deep southern accent and an aristocrat's love of bloodlines, though he was not a snob at all. Everybody to whom he spoke he drew into his strange, fey circle. He himself issued from two of the wealthiest bloodlines in the South, the Duke line and the Burns. I had spent many afternoons with him in our office, listening to his accounts of the old days—the balls, the concerts, the evening salons where culture bloomed among them like a beautiful virus spreading, making them feel their souls sprouting within them in that way only the extraordinarily rich have the time to do. The balls seemed to have been fantastic, gruesome affairs. Money meets money, in the form of young people, and begins that slow, blossom-saturated dance unto marriage.

His largesse notwithstanding, Mr. Burns was about to go on trial for fraud, specifically real estate fraud, involving a deal three years ago in the Carolinas. Today, standing in front of me, he vaguely bowed. "I wonder," he said, "if you would be so kind as to write a letter to the judge regarding my character. I think it would help if he saw my business partners were behind me."

"Of course," I said, though you couldn't in one million years call us his business partners. We were the recipients and sometimes the victims of his erratic generosity. He gave and then took away such that we always felt his tyranny over our lives. Often he'd give us too much money and then need to take some back for a time. So the Noodle House rose and fell on the basis of his whims, on whatever sense he had of himself and his generosity from month to month. In the interest of full disclosure, I should say that I did know at times that Mr. Burns needed to use Aquinas to perform some complicated financial maneuvers. I would never have thought of it quite as money laundering, but I suppose I should have. I guess I turned a kind of blind eye to what he might have been doing, but in my defense, really, no charity investigates fully the reasons behind its benefactors' gifts. That would be foolhardy. Even Mother Teresa—she took her money from Pol Pot, from Duvalier. Most money has at one time passed through hands so rotten that all of it is compromised. All of it is smoke rising out of a beautiful, burning forest.

7

James did call. After a long rain, late on a Thursday afternoon. I was at the office, staring into the wet, checkered heart of Soho. Peter was looking over some student sketches, unrolling them noisily, sighing, writing down little notes on his steno pad. I thought he was being a little self-important about the class he was teaching this semester; it was his first, and perhaps it was hard to resist feeling a bit full of yourself, all those trusting undergraduates writing down your casual bon mots, treasuring even your vaguest, least-formed ideas.

"Justine!" James said when I said hello.

"James," I said.

"Hi."

"Where are you?"

"I'm here," he said. "I'm in the city." Some pigeons took flight from our window ledges into the sinking dusk. I knew that within the hour I'd be seeing him. With him the time elapsing between the call and the meeting had always been very brief—he'd be on foot in an instant, tracking along the quad with a paperback under his arm, Walter Benjamin, Wittgenstein, Solzhenitsyn, or his by-far favorite at the time, Madame de Staël, muse to Emerson and Thoreau.

Today we agreed to meet at the South Street Seaport, and soon I was stepping onto its main street, which was like entering a different city, the only reminder of New York the great, pointed shadow of the bridge. Here were suddenly tiny, cobbled seaside streets leading toward the silted river. On either side of the street, little chichi shops and upscale restaurants were opening up, but they could never overcome the magnificent brininess and disrepute of the area, all of it cast in a lime light, everything always crystallizing, crusting at the edges, the shadows of rats darting everywhere, trailing their elaborate histories, from Casablanca, from the coasts of Norway and Spain. I saw James in profile, against the rail as he said he would be.

"Justine," he said when I reached him. He smiled, and we hugged; he was wearing a shirt that I recognized, unbelievably, just an old red T-shirt that had been threadbare even ten years earlier. Beyond him the water flowed on, the East River. And above his left shoulder the moon was already shining. This was what I'd always imagined of heaven—the calm, ordinary greeting with somebody who has lived only inside your mind for years, the earth still visible but palely over his shoulder, the desires one had there still relevant but less insistent.

For dinner, we wound our way up through Chinatown—Mott, Canal, Grand—and he told me something of his script, about a superhero, a reporter who, when he feels too much sympathy for a situation, turns into a woman, a Wonder Woman–type woman. Wow, I thought as we ducked in and out of the crowds, chandeliers of squid and octopuses dangling over our heads, the smell of Asia—smoke and salt—everywhere. "I wouldn't necessarily expect a script like that from you," I said. I recalled him writing poetry about ravines and outcroppings and knotty roots along a forest floor, that sort of thing.

"Nor I," he said.

"Are you exploring your own feminine side?" I asked.

"Always," said James.

He did have a long-running interest in the classics, especially Ovid, and I thought perhaps this character could be considered a modern-day permutation of Ovid—*My intention is to tell of bodies changed to different forms!*

"Is it called *Woman-Man*?" I asked.

"I wish! It's called *Harvest*."

"That's a beautiful title," I said.

"Thanks, I hope it sticks. The studio thinks I'm focusing too much on the setting, and there's not enough action."

"Ah. Well, I've always thought there was too much action in movies."

James laughed. "I know, and there's never enough setting."

"Everything's just setting, if you think about it, people are ornamental." We were heading up toward Little Italy, and James stopped at a corner vendor to buy a little bag of those sugar nuts whose steam was ubiquitous on the city streets. My friend Bonnie-Beth called them evil nuts. I'd never actually seen a person purchase or eat them, but James was now pouring a bag of them into his mouth. He tilted his head up, and that gesture lit up an abandoned little circuit in my mind. I could never have called it forth on my own, but once he did it, I saw him do it a thousand times in memory, throwing his head back to take a drink, or to look at the Cambridge night sky, or in exasperation. A friend gets stored there, deep in the mind, and quietly waits, giving peace and good judgment to one's life, shedding light from down in the depths.

8

The end of September in New York City took a turn toward the very hot and humid, one long, last flashback to summer. For weeks I'd meant to mention to Peter the reappearance of James, my old friend, but then there wasn't an appropriate time, and anyway I'd forgotten why it was necessary to bring it up at all. Peter and I rarely shared personal matters with each other; we just eventually absorbed them by proximity. On this night, the air was still very warm and a little fragrant—a hint of Tiananmen maybe, due to the evil nuts roasting and the lotus blossoms for sale outside Carnegie Hall, where the Beijing Opera was performing for five nights. The smell of the lotus is just slightly rotten at the height of its bloom, beautiful but with something terrible running through its perfume. I was with Peter, but we weren't really speaking much. You could do this with him— lose yourself in his silence. Plus the Beijing Opera is always so bewildering, there's hardly anything to say at all, during or after. If you knew nothing of human life and then came to the Beijing Opera, you would leave believing existence on earth to be almost entirely discordant—an off-kilter mix of will and desire and duty, all topping out in madness.

The audience had been full of people Peter and I knew quite well—lots of China experts and charity people that we wanted to avoid, including my ex-boyfriend, a tall, irritating man, his head above the crowd. I saw him as soon as we entered the hall. I had dated him briefly three years ago in Princeton, New Jersey, where he and I were both working for Shelter the Children. And then, in a stunning display of bad judgment, I had re-dated him in New York City. At any rate, in trying to avoid him we ran right into him at a little bodega next door, into which Peter and I had ducked for some cigarettes and wine gums after the performance.

"Christopher," I said.

"Justine. Peter. Hi." He was buying a *Newsweek* and a pack of gum. He was wearing a tux. "Just the people."

"You enjoyed it?" Peter asked.

"I suppose. Look, I was going to call you two. I'm going to Rwanda as soon as I can get clearance. I wondered if Aquinas could donate twenty or so of those lean-tos."

I knew the last thing Peter wanted to do was throw any support behind Christopher, but we had about four hundred of these lean-tos Peter had designed in a warehouse on the Upper East Side, none of them being used currently. He'd designed a somewhat revolutionary lean-to years ago, and it was now standard issue around the world for medical supplies and treatment in times of crisis. I'd stood in many of them myself; they were like efficient, elegant little machines, letting in the wind and the sun and the rain in all the right amounts, suggesting shelter yet also a kind of openness and ease, so that people would feel more inclined to approach. The lean-tos folded up like huge folding chairs when everything was done, the revolution cast aside or the drought relieved. Peter had designed them based on an elegant, collapsible cardboard shelter he'd seen a homeless guy building down in Battery Park. We were both very proud of them, but neither of us was dying to help out Christopher. He was one of those insane charity people you hear about, who hustle off to trouble spots as if they're big parties he's missing. These were the early days of the Rwandan exodus. It was already playing on every television set around the city—the people walking endlessly over the border. Christopher would be there soon; one couldn't help but picture him still in his ridiculous tux, waving at the last cameras. It's not that he was ineffective; in fact, he was incredibly effective—tireless, warmhearted, eager, gregarious—but under the surface there was always just the slight suggestion that he was doing all this good for the wrong reasons: that is, his own PR reasons, and actually, more insidiously than that, his own internal PR, the things he broadcast about himself to himself.

"Give us a call," Peter said, suddenly magnanimous. "We'll arrange it." I nodded in agreement, and we all waved good-bye.

"I can't believe you dated that guy," Peter said a minute later, as we were turning onto Broadway. We'd decided to walk a little, until we had to fork off in different directions at Twenty-third. "I know," I said as I swallowed a Xanax, which I always took as I walked south on Broadway, in preparation for my arrival home. The previous year, I think I'd dated Christopher mostly because of Peter's reaction, which wasn't exactly jealous, mostly just dismissive and slightly sarcastic, but it was enough of a show of feeling for me to at least try to take it romantically. But in my defense, the first time I'd become interested in Christopher—in Princeton—I was incredibly bored with charity work, day after day in Shelter's concrete warehouse, processing nonfund aid, which involved mostly sorting through what had been donated, trying to discern and separate out what was actually useful. A lot of this work, at least at my end of the warehouse, involved sorting through shipments of drugs. Pharmaceutical companies were notorious for sending us junk aid; any drugs that had been sitting on the shelf for too long they contributed to charities for the tax write-off. I spent whole days sifting through cases of Diflucan, Tavist-D, Clorazil, Depo-Provera, Minoxidil, reading labels and trying to decide if anybody in the crisis zones, in Bengal, in

Mozambique, could really use acne medicine or hair-growing schemes.

One company donated a huge shipment of Dexatrim, which was actually an appetite suppressant, a precursor to Fen-Phen, intended for Somalia. It was probably just mindless, their sending it, but it seemed cruelly so. We joked that perhaps in a place where people were routinely starving to death, an appetite suppressant could serve as a painkiller of sorts. At any rate, it was into this situation that Christopher stepped. He was in charge of operations in Somalia and the greater part of East Africa, and he seemed to me so vital and alive, and his enthusiasm for charity work struck me as genuine and impressive, and in addition, he seemed himself both dashing and incorruptible. But this would have been a lot to explain to Peter, and anyway, we had reached the point on Broadway where he forked off to take the subway to Brooklyn and I continued on to my apartment in the Village. The place we always said good-bye, coming from uptown, was this worn-down spot, where an all-night bagel shop shed its purply light all over us.

"Bye," I said. "I see you." This was what Yiang-Yang always said when she hung up the phone. He leaned over to kiss my cheek. He was so polite, his hand on my shoulder, his face close to mine. Though he maintained a formality toward me (and everybody really) at all times, it was never cold. He had many loves. I could easily list them: the Cambodian countryside, Pol Pot's daughter, his twenty-years-dead girlfriend Su Chen Xian, the mountains of North Carolina and Tennessee, movies about World War II, which was the war in which two of his uncles died brilliantly, baguettes of bread, roasted chickens, French wines, his litchi nuts, bonsai trees, the waterfalls of South Africa, the Western Wall, Quebeçois accents, redwoods in Northern California, a small nephew by the name of Bucky, who lived in the Deep South and sent letters regularly, and then, in truth, my own family right here in New York City, my own parents, so much so that at times I felt too weirdly familial with him to be in love with him. And I was worried always that this might be how he felt about me, that he believed my affections were those of a small, niece-type person now grown up and working for him. But here we are, I thought, back in America. Why don't we just begin the long chain of events that, looked back on, equals a romance? Would that be the end of the world, would that be so bad?

9

There was more bad news pouring in from China; the next morning Yiang-Yang sent in a fax stating that the proposal for the extension was moving past the lower courts already, to what the Chinese called their magistrate. The proposal was for a five-thousand-foot addition to the dam. There was a terrible clause attached, which very elegantly eliminated all of our hopes and dreams. It said there would be no foreign reparations, which meant that those of us who had land beside and overlooking the Yangtze would still own the land, although it would be under thirty-five feet of water. We were suddenly in the company of those persons who owned swamplands or wetlands or old sunken riverbeds.

The money for the Noodle House came from many sources, but quite a lot of it came from Mr. Burns. And though it wouldn't have been right to blame Mr. Burns for the Three Gorges Dam, which had been in the planning stages since the time of Emperor Sun Yat-sen, I couldn't help but notice that everything Mr. Burns touched was exquisite for one second and then disappeared forever.

I guess it's not accurate to say that the land would vanish entirely; it would just, once the dam was operating, be at the bottom of the Yangtze, in fact, *be* the bottom of the Yangtze, the bed of the Yangtze, the place where the nearly extinguished white river dolphin touched its belly on its way in and out again, the ground of the great China bottom-walker fish, which walked about the earth but underwater. Instead of hosting the Noodle House with all its fabulous celebrities and rich people in search of peace, that land would be a quiet world, roiling with silent life—blood lobsters, underwater butterflies, eels shivering through green, blurry luxuries of seaweed.

"I can be sorry," Yiang-Yang had scrawled along the bottom of the fax.

10

The next morning, a cool, bright day, I was stepping into the shadows of the Southern District Courthouse. I was hand-delivering a letter attesting to Mr. Burns's character and generosity to the judge presiding over the case. Since the trial was already in session, after I passed off the letter to a secretary, I slipped into one of the back rows to watch for a while.

Mr. Burns had set up a small artistic community down in the Carolinas, on a particularly wild, changing edge of the Atlantic, at the place where the Cape Fear River empties into the sea. He'd sold a little community of about twelve quixotic, sunstruck cabins on spindly stilts to various artists—novelists, painters, potters, actors, musicians—most of them from New York City. In addition, there was a main building, also on stilts, where in the evenings the artists gathered and performed for one another. I'd gone there one weekend with him when he was feeling particularly unbalanced and felt he needed a traveling companion. He had behaved, as far as I could see, like a looming, dysfunctional father, but the artists seemed to endure him and even loved him in a grudging way.

The whole compound was surrounded by palm trees, and so close to the ocean that at high tide the shoreline infiltrated it, gently gathering around the ankles of those on foot, and from inside the cabins it seemed kind of mystical, to be living like that, in the ocean's outermost realm. Of course these buildings had been about to fall into the sea. This had been apparent even to the untrained eye. Perhaps Mr. Burns hadn't told this to the artists directly, but they should have noticed. I was surprised actually that the place lasted as long as it did—over three years. But after a few intersections of the high tide with the full moon, and three small hurricanes, the houses came down, crouching at first like injured, long-legged animals, then fully kneeling, bowing, their shoulders to the earth. The photographs of the buildings that now hung at the front of the courtroom, as the prosecution built its case, were vivid reminders that everything is brought to its knees, everything except the sea. I thought this was exactly the kind of lesson artists were always trying to learn, and I believed they should all have cut their losses and run.

As I settled into the courtroom, the plaintiff's attorney, a scrappy and handsome man with a little ponytail, by the name of Leonard Keen, was building his case, talking with a novelist from the Midwest, a bearded, trim man, who I actu-

ally remembered meeting during a visit down South. He
had given a reading from his novel, something about a ship-
builder, and I had thought it lovely. On the stand the novelist was describing the day Mr. Burns first took him to the
compound. Apparently, the sun had been slanting into the
waves, and the novelist said a deep peace overtook him. He
said he thought all the moments in his life had led to this
beautiful place, that it was his destiny. I recognized this as a
feeling one often had around Mr. Burns. All his property
had this quality; one was meant to sacrifice everything to be
there. Mr. Burns happened also to own three buildings in
New York City, including the one in which our office was located. Our rent was extraordinarily cheap, and the view
from our windows was stunning, all of the southern shore
of Manhattan offered to the imagination. The room itself
was so intelligently conceived. It was built in the 1880s by an
architect who committed suicide in the early days of the
next century. I suppose the same emotional oversensitivity
that had eventually done him in had also come up with our
room. It was expansive and intimate both. The southern
wall was a bank of windows, angled outward, like the prow
of a ship. One expected that any day she might pick herself
up and head down West Broadway, go thudding into the
nighttime seas. Also, Mr. Burns seemed to believe that nothing ever ought to be repaired, that to repair too much was to
intrude on time's hopes and dreams for the material world,

and so the building was essentially falling apart. Outside our windows was a small balcony whose balustrade was torn away completely, so that you couldn't help feeling a little worried at all times. When I'd stood inside one of the cabins in North Carolina, I'd been visited with that same feeling, a kind of quiet imbalance which indicated, just in case you hadn't noticed, that nothing lasts forever. Mr. Burns would give you the world, but he would also extract from you a certain peace of mind. Some days it felt like I would one day be patching together the office myself, plastering and repairing, and this eventually would be my only task, beating back the waves, which in New York City were not salt water of course, but of a quieter nature, of simple air and time.

11

I returned to our office in the rain, took the shaking elevator up. Peter greeted me at the door and kissed me gallantly on the cheek, which made me suspicious. He led me to his desk, where there was yet another of his sketches for the Noodle House. I shuddered inwardly; any new plan shattered our finances, which were holding steady at present, but just barely. Though technically I worked for Peter, it had evolved that he needed my approval on matters that would increase or change the budget, which were all matters. It was left to me always to say yes or no. In reality, I said only yes. Yes, yes, always yes.

Regarding this particular revision, however, we had an ongoing disagreement. Peter had been insisting that the ceiling heights vary significantly from room to room, and I'd been dragging my heels, since making this happen would cost close to an additional fifty thousand dollars. I thought I'd squelched him already on this score, but I saw now he had returned to it. I had to admit the plans were lovelier this way—tiny, gemlike rooms, faceted and perfectly themselves. Each of these rooms had a maker, and even their sketchy little existences bore witness to this.

The building, as Peter saw it, was to address as completely as possible the emotional needs of a person, to restore to her some interest in the measure of what a person is—the ceilings in the bedrooms closing in to suggest intimacy and privacy and those in the communal rooms pulling back up to suggest largesse toward others, toward crowds, toward one's community of friends.

Sometimes it crossed my mind that Peter had too much belief in his ability to affect human passions with his rooms, to catch the gears of a person's heart as she stepped from one room to another. I glimpsed it only now and then, a kind of hubris that sprang out of charity, a desire to make the world perfect rather than to provide shelter from imperfection.

"So," he said.

"Okay." Yes again. I set out that afternoon to make it possible, budget-wise. Fifty thousand was on the borderline between an amount large enough that one had to go find it and elicit it from somebody, and an amount that one could have in a matter of hours if one could just think hard enough while crunching the numbers, attempting to look at what one had differently. I chose the latter, but it ended up taking all day, until Peter and I stepped out onto Houston

Street, at about seven o'clock, to go eat some Chinese food. The sun was setting in such a way that the buildings appeared plated with zinc or bronze, and they in turn cast a beautiful light onto the street, interpreting all passersby as brief, vanishing flames.

You will live in seaside and hilltop resorts for life, was my fortune that night, after a long meal of noodles, pork loin, and green onion.

"I wonder when that will begin," Peter said. He leaned back expansively. "Do you want to come with me Sunday night, to Zhou's book signing? It's at that little bookstore in Chinatown, across from the statue." The statue was of Confucius, made of a greeny marble, facing the river and Brooklyn beyond. Zhou was Peter's best friend and was publishing a monograph about the friendship between Li Po and Tu Fu, two poets from the Tang Dynasty.

"I can't," I said. "I'm eating at my parents' place." I normally ate dinner with them on Sunday nights, and this weekend James was joining me. "I'm going to his reading at NYU, though. I'll be there."

"Ah well, you're busy bee. Bzzzz." When Peter said things like this to me, I thought I could feel the faintest suggestion of malice, or ridicule. Was I oversensitive? Probably, but maybe my oversensitivity allowed me to spy out some secret hostility in him. When you love somebody as I loved Peter—unrequitedly—it becomes necessary to watch him very closely, and this vigilance brings up all sorts of unpleasant un- or even nontruths.

"Say hello to your parents from me," he said.

"Oh I will," I said, but probably I wouldn't. I had to bring up Peter very gingerly to my parents. They loved him, though my mother in particular felt that I was wasting my life waiting for him to get over Su Chen. It was her belief that all of his strangeness and aloofness, even his diabetes, was owing to his feelings of guilt over Su Chen's death. Whether guilt had the power to trip up one's blood sugar seemed very open to debate, but my mother was sure of it, and also sure that Peter could never be rehabilitated. She was always asking me to please date somebody else soon. Of course it doesn't take a mother to know that it's impossible to do battle, romantically, with a dead person.

But in 1983, when Peter had just moved back to New York City to start up Aquinas, I returned home one snowy weekend from college to find him in my parents' living room. I had no idea he'd be there. I dropped my duffel bag in the front hall and peeked in the living room to say hi, and there he was, lifting his head from some photographs my mother was showing him. I was twenty-one years old then, and my emotional life was overactive enough to build an entire life in the moments that Peter lifted his head and I recognized him as *Peter*, Su Chen's Peter, and mine. I thought we would resume our life—their life—and the two of us together would be all we would need of home—a cozy, warm, compact, serene, and glamorous home, invisible but real, surrounding us as we traveled.

I came home frequently after that on the weekends and saw him often—usually just coffee or the movies. And during the weeks I didn't come home, I would sit in my room on Brattle Street in Cambridge, its ornate windows with their blurry, imperceptibly sliding glass giving way to the blossoming beauty of Boston in the springtime, and imagine Peter, high on the Upper West Side, where he lived, taking his solitary evening walks along the wide open boulevards, veering into the dark, inviting, and cool lanes of Riverside Park, every part of him mysterious to me, unavailable.

12

My parents lived on Central Park West, in the same apartment we had moved into after our years in China. Together they ran an organization called Open Gate, which was designed to help people who were moving to New York City from other countries, with special but not exclusive emphasis on refugees. Both my parents were trust-fund babies, both rich from the get-go, raised in happy, wealthy Midwestern families (my mother's money came from a Norwegian shipping company, my father's from various oil booms in this century), and this had freed up their lives to do pretty much as they pleased, within reason. My father had become a missionary as a young man, and my mother had been a stewardess for Pan-Am in the sixties, back when people still dressed up to take flights, and stewardesses wore white leather go-go boots to right below their knees. After they fell in love, my mother trailed along for a while as a missionary herself, but never really had the heart for it. Her thinking on religion was too speculative. She was very much at peace with faith itself, and didn't much care to turn it into certainty.

Tonight my mother and James and I sat on our small balcony, waiting for the other guests to arrive. My father had gone to pick them up, a Hmong family by the name of Tran. I tried to fill James in briefly on their recent journey to this country, beginning in a bamboo hut in Laos and through a refugee camp in Thailand from which they departed in a spectacular escape—over an electrical fence and down the side of a sheer rock face. The family was composed of one father, two daughters, and one grandbaby, who was two months old at the time of escape and had been sewn into a pillowy bodysuit the women of the camp had quilted for him, made of old rags filled with pollen and dust. He was tossed up over a fence and then dangled over the cliff's edge, up hundreds of feet alone, waiting, while the rest of his family scrambled and fell—bleeding, breaking various limbs—down to him.

The family had thought New York City would be their final destination, though once they'd arrived here they'd realized there was a deeper paradise, that the city was a false bottom, and the place they needed to go ultimately was Minnesota—heavenly place of unlimited kindness and beauty stretching across the middle of the country, its beautiful high cornfields, its pastures of large animals grazing, its pulsating northern lights—the place where many Hmong had quit their roving, quit their mountains, and found peace.

So there was a strategy to the night. My mother had also invited Francis Efferveti, an old missionary friend of theirs from China, who currently worked in refugee relief at the U.N. She was hoping he could help the family relocate.

But for now, my mother was very happy to see James after all these years; she had always liked him. The outdoor lamps and candles cast a buzzy light across her face and dress, which was a Kandinsky-like design, circa 1965, and she was wrapped in a shawl. She was the only woman I knew who still wore wigs—coppery, burnished Mary Tyler Moore–type wigs. The air tonight was beautiful—cold, resistant, happy, and powerful enough I'd noticed on the way here to already snap some leaves off their trees. Below us the great rectangle of the park stretched forward darkly, fringed by the bright blur of traffic, the car horns reaching us but dimly on the seventeenth floor. I could smell the duck roasting in his silver pan. I knew from experience that this duck had hung outside our living room windows for six hours this afternoon, struck through its back and wings with a chopstick, drying out in the fall afternoon sunlight. To make Peking duck, you need a very dead duck, one who has no remnant of its formerly coursing life at all, so that you can then re-saturate it with sherry and vinegar and honey, and give back to the duck all it has lost.

I looked through our sliding glass doors and saw the great warmth of our home, its wall hangings from the Gambia, from New Guinea, from Mongolia, all the places my parents had taken the Gospel, only to surrender to those places, their own gods and ways. My parents had gone so far afield to share what they believed was the truth, and once they got there the truth as they knew it had always, every time, shattered, and they had been good enough to enjoy this and bring it home, in little statuettes of the Buddha, batiks of the nine-armed Krishna, a Nigerian bead shaker to ward away the demons of the afterworld.

"James," my mother said, "I remember those wonderful poems you used to write. Justine always brought them home from college, and I thought they were so good."

"Oh dear," James said. "Thank you. That's nice of you."

"There was one about an eye tearing up that was so precious to me. And then one about some gulls over Hatteras."

"Well, thank you for remembering," he said.

"Will you publish a book of poems?"

"I don't think so, no," he said.

"He's making movies now, Mom," I said. "You don't go back to poetry after movies."

"I don't see why not."

My father was now walking toward us through the apartment with the Hmong family. My parents loved their work with Open Gate—setting up apartments for new families, helping them meet people once they were in New York, taking care of all sorts of paperwork, leases and green cards and schooling and such, and then in general hovering over these often totally discombobulated people, who were almost always grateful to be here, some of them having passed through such versions of hell that by the time I met them they seemed like superheroes to me: Dakan Tor! Brave Cambodian who disemboweled himself in front of Margaret Thatcher in the Hong Kong camps, and lived to tell. Or Isabel Santino, who refused to give birth until her boat touched dry land. Or this little guy coming over tonight, who had been hung over the earth, twirling, suspended, for half a day.

These days my mother was very focused on the two teenage Hmong girls, who had lost their mother in the refugee camp. My mother was now obsessively mothering them, to the point of divesting my old closet of all my clothes, including an electric-blue satin sleeveless prom dress and a ruffly green bridesmaid's dress with a big black bow on the rear (1983). She'd also given them a little stacked set of Chinese dolls and all my Holly Hobbies, as well as an old and stern-looking Indonesian puppet that had hung in my window all through my childhood and that frankly I was happy to see go as it had always looked unhappy and judgmental of my messy room and life.

We were already seated around the crackling, burnished

duck, all of us just nodding and smiling across the language barrier, when Francis arrived. He had fled Beijing about a year after we did, and had worked at the UN since then, though I didn't see how given his messianic and extreme views on every issue. In fact, I was even surprised that my parents had managed to stay close to him as he was so conservative, an old-timey missionary man who believed very explicitly that life on earth matters only to the extent that it prepares one for heaven. He pulled up a seat, half-bowing, wearing a dark sweater and dark slacks, his jet-black hair slicked back for a night out. He smiled at everybody curtly, nodded to me, *hello, Dolly* (this had been his name for me in China), and I was reminded that I liked him quite a bit. He seemed to understand that he cut a very anachronistic, almost comical figure, and he took this well.

As soon as he sat down, my mother started talking to him about the family going to Minnesota. The family hardly spoke any English so my mother spoke on their behalf. "Well, the Hmong like to roam," Francis said. "They're not settlers. They never want to stop."

"This family does want to settle," my mother said. "They want to go to Minnesota, where the rest of their family is."

"The Hmong are a stubborn people," he said.

I was about to protest this, but I saw that the patriarch of the family, who maybe understood the meaning of this statement, looked quite proud.

The baby had been placed in a car seat on top of the long table, facing down the duck. I noticed him looking at me for a long time, which was unnerving. I stared back at him. He raised an eyebrow and looked around the apartment—*Central Park West, eh?* he seemed to say.

What?

Nice place to grow up. Cushy.

I was as innocent as you as a baby. I didn't choose wealth for myself.

He shrugged it off. *Sure.*

Look, just because I didn't hang along a cliff's edge!

He looked very imperiously at me. He was wearing a hat with some intricate Laplander-type stitching across the brow and a red pom-pom on top. And then I noticed a slight twitch of his lower lip, and within one moment he was crying furiously.

Impressively, James leapt into action, waving his hands in front of the baby's face. "Are you the Fresh Prince? I think you're the Fresh Prince. You're the Fresh Prince."

The baby calmed instantly, turning his attention to James.

"Francis, come on now," my mother was saying, as he launched into another one of his mini-sermons about do-gooders ruining the lives of the poor by helping them rather than letting them find their own way. He quoted a verse in the Bible about Jesus stilling the waters, the point of which turned out to be that people should just calm down, accept their lot, and worship God. Of course, there were many exceptions to this in Francis's life, people he had valiantly tried to help, most notably Su Chen. In 1971, the worst of Mao's offenses were still underreported in China and even in the United States. Only a small handful of people were speaking out against Mao publicly, and one of these people was Francis. He had immunity, of course, because he could leave China at any moment, but still, it was true that he had spoken out about the problem with Mao much earlier than anybody else. As well, he had found a post-doc for Su Chen at Oxford University in comparative literature, then a relatively new field. But instead, Su Chen, at Peter's urging, had stayed in China, and accepted a position in Zhongnanhai, with an organization called The Cultural Work Troupe, a group of young future leaders handpicked by Mao to study inside the Forbidden City.

I knew Peter found it very painful to think about the other possibilities for Su Chen's life, roads she hadn't taken, and that he had prevented her from pursuing. I said a silent prayer of thanks that I hadn't invited Peter to dinner tonight.

"And how is your work with Peter's so-called charity?" Francis asked.

"Fine, except our project basically went underwater this month. They're about to vote, I think, to extend the dam, just a little bit, but enough to eradicate our land."

"Oh, honey," my mother said. "You're kidding."

My father whistled. "How is Peter taking it?"

"He doesn't know yet. I haven't told him. I don't want to alarm him before I know for sure."

My mother was an excellent cook, but she had a couple of blind spots, I thought. After the beautiful, nearly gold-plated duck, she served her famous no-sugar, not-very-tasty cinnamon yogurt. So, as in childhood, I ate about twenty-five After-Eight mints in an effort to approximate dessert. In addition, after we left their apartment, James and I stopped off along Ninth Avenue at the Dipping Dots, which was just new and looked to be a concept so good it was going to take over the world.

"Thanks for coming," I said to James after we ordered the ice cream. "That was a sort of weird dinner."

"Oh, thank you. I loved it. Baudrillard would have something to say about it."

"Hmmm?"

"He spoke of the joy of language, apart from meaning."

"Ah!"

"Though wasn't that gross when Francis kept referring to the UN as a secular organ."

"I know. I saw your face. Very immature of you."

"He looks like Get Smart."

"He does. He just has that one suit."

"He might be the worst person I've ever met. I thought

he was going to try to baptize me when he found out I hadn't been."

"You really should be," I said. "Just to be safe." We were back on the street, meandering west through the midnight crowds, eating the Dots, which were the perfect food really, small, soft, pastel ball bearings rolling around in the mouth. Some jazz music from Lincoln Center floated, distorted, nearby. "What if you get hit by a car tonight, on the next block?"

"Well, it's off to hell with me then," he said.

13

According to some principle of control through chaos, the Chinese government kept the time and place of its decisions secret so that whenever a vote came down it was with a thundering blow to whomever it affected. Which was why Yiang-Yang with her hundreds of connections in the government nevertheless did not find out about the date of the final vote regarding the Yangtze until the night before, which was a Thursday. I was in bed; she called me at home. She seemed quite calm about it, though Yiang-Yang could seem calm about anything. She was one of those women Mao spoke of whose head holds up the world. She had passed through in her thirty years any number of difficult situations. She had been born in 1963, one of those babies born to mothers while they worked, amid the barley and grasses, her first breath clogged with the beautiful, sunlit dust of the fields. It must have been psychedelic to break into the world in the outdoors, into Asia, the color of sky and wheat, the rough texture of stalks, and then to be brought up to her mother's face, tied in a sling and carried, her mother bending and planting, bending and planting, through the day's work, her mother calling out to the other women, "I have named her Yiang-Yang."

So on an overcast morning, the sky changing by seconds from silver to gray, I made my way to our office and checked our answering machine—one message from an IRS agent in charge of Aquinas's returns, a man we disliked and feared beyond measure, and one from an unidentified woman asking for Peter. I was trying to construct a woman around the voice as I pulled out the one fax from overnight, which said, simply, irreversibly, that the National People's Congress had at last approved the extension to the dam. "They approved it," Yiang-Yang had written. "The dam will be extended." Though the Noodle House had been a long time in the falling, this final blow to it registered very slowly in my brain. And at last, I think I pictured the Noodle House perhaps as corporeally as Peter had all along. In the few seconds before it fell, I saw it racing along the Yangtze, its height suggesting contentment and its movement along the horizon suggesting desire. In this way, according to Peter, a well-designed building pays its respects to the human frame, in which stillness and desire mingle so profoundly.

At the bottom of the fax, Yiang-Yang had written, *You must call me whenever is now.* The fax was on the desk in front of me when Peter walked in. I slid it under some books as he approached and touched my upper back, the vertebrae directly below the neck. He went to kiss me hello. I was suffering from the kind of minor paralysis great feeling can bring about, so could not even tilt my head upward to accept his kiss. Therefore it landed in the hollow of my temple as I stared out at the city, at our little portion of it, the long granite canyons of Soho. Peter's hand was cool, his blood sugar low. Now was not quite the time. He passed immediately on to his sketches, sketching and eating granola intermittently. He'd been preoccupied the past few days with the gate that would open onto the main lane, lined by ginkgoes and leading toward the Noodle House.

"What do you think?" he said after a while. He had sketched a gate of black wrought iron with a subtle Asian cast, about eight feet high, through which you could see the Noodle House. The heart of the design was a complicated circle, through which the main door—a rich, warm, exotic red—was visible.

"Looks fine," I said.

"You don't like it?"

"I like it fine." My guilt over letting him work on this doomed project for even one more moment seemed to be expressing itself as hostility.

"See, outside you feel humility, the sense that you are one among many things, but then you step inside and feel at once a sense of your own worth. And the gate is the transition between those two states."

I tried to nod in acknowledgment, but it was halfhearted, and then turned back to my work, some grant forms that were so beside the point emotionally that I could barely make out what information they were trying to extract from me, let alone begin the manipulation of truth and projection of fantasy that is great writing.

"I've noticed this about you," he said. "You don't have any real interest in the threshold."

"I do so."

"Seem not to."

"I love the threshold." I nearly blurted out that the threshold was soon to be under fourteen feet of water, so what matter who loves what?

I didn't do much the rest of the day except, hour upon hour, nearly tell Peter of the extension to the dam. I definitely needed to tell him before he heard it over the news. It seemed like something that might be reported on the BBC, which he listened to nightly as he fell asleep. Finally, I gathered my tiny share of courage and lifted my head to tell him, but then I spied the orange autumn moon already out over the angel of City Hall. It's too late, I thought. I had told Bonnie-Beth I would meet her by seven. I did make one last stab while I put on my coat.

"Do you want to have drinks tonight?" I asked Peter.

"You mean now?"

Now would have been customary. Later had other, richer

associations. Ordinarily I wouldn't have suggested this, but Peter's thinking I might have romantic designs was now the least of my worries.

"Later," I said. "How about eleven or so, Washington Square? There's something I want to discuss with you."

"Okay," he said. "I'm going to a movie at nine-fifteen, though, so could we make it eleven-thirty?"

"You have a date?" I asked.

"At my age," he said, "you don't have dates, you have walkabouts, where the two of you survey the changes in the skyline."

He meant this to be amusing, but nevertheless this sight— Peter and a distinguished woman, their blazing silver hair, making their way through the city, discussing it in their arch, compassionate ways—dismayed me. The childish desire to be older had not left me, even now that I was in my thirties. I had always believed that the difference in our ages would shrink with time in his mind, but this had not as of yet happened. I rode the elevator down and walked out into the darkening air of Manhattan. There were leaves everywhere on Houston, but hardly any trees to be seen, another of the street's mysteries. Also, there was in the air an unmistakable saltiness mixed with the cold. The sea in fall changes as spectacularly as the land, and this can be felt even this far inland—the invisible, palpable spray. Even in the middle of Broadway, its lights careening through the crowds, we were breathing in and out the sea. It was always here, as I crossed over Broadway, between Houston and Bleecker, with the great church ahead and Chinatown behind, that I thought most closely of Peter, wondered what various intonations of his words and phrases had indicated, how completely his heart, over all these years, may or may not have developed an immunity to me.

I knew that romantically I was invisible to him, but sometimes I thought that this might eventually work in my favor, that one day he might lift his head, and here I'd be, as close as air, as sure, as necessary.

14

⁓

I was meeting Bonnie-Beth at a restaurant called Cu-
viendu's, which was a very homey little hole-in-the-wall we
had heard about from Bonnie-Beth's friend Cinnamon. It
was across the street from an ornate Russian onion-dome
church on the edge of the West Village. Hanging in the window of the restaurant was a flag that neither of us could
place—three broad stripes; blue, yellow, red, with a coat of
arms inside the yellow—until we went inside and found
that the walls were covered with photos of Ceausescu and
his wife, Elena.

"Romania!" Bonnie-Beth said.

This was four years after the Revolution, after the Ceausescus had been shot via firing squad on Christmas Day
1989 (that incredible year that included Tiananmen and the
fall of the Berlin Wall). The footage had been so startling,
especially to see a woman—the well-dressed, high-heeled,
and merciless Elena—crumpling to her knees, her face
falling into her lap.

But here were apparently some very rare supporters of the Ceausescus. Our waiter brought us each a vodka, which was so strong it was like a shot of tear gas. Every membrane in my face seemed to dissolve when the alcohol hit it.

"Damn," Bonnie-Beth said. "Thank God I'm not still pregnant."

I looked up and searched her face immediately. Bonnie-Beth had miscarried two months earlier, and I was on the alert at all times for signs that she was suffering. I knew she was sad but I never knew how much I should inquire after her feelings. She changed the subject herself. "How's old Lamplighter?"

"He's fine." That was her name for Peter because he had once wanted to call the charity Lamplighter. "I'm meeting him after dinner," I said.

Bonnie-Beth, to me, was a nearly perfect person—precise, intelligent, intrepid, organized, with a stubbornness so good-hearted you only really find it in children anymore. I had met her at a fund-raiser for Riverkeeper (she herself ran a nonprofit called River Doctors), and I had loved her immediately, friendship at first sight. She was like a character from a novel—Dorothea, maybe, or Emma, or Jane Eyre. She had something of the plucky, old-fashioned girl to her, and I had recognized her at once from my reading life.

She also had a husband at home named Charles—Chuck—who was like a bear, a big, friendly, quiet beast that clomped contentedly around their apartment. He was a whole different take on a husband, and I'd actually seen the light dawn in women's eyes when they met him—this was a direction they hadn't thought to take. But since Chuck was nearly silent most of the time, Bonnie-Beth also saw a therapist, mostly I thought to have some regular male conversation. Tonight she began to report to me Dr. Michael's newest "technique" for getting past an unhealthy habit, which involved drawing an imaginary string between the bad habit and the part of yourself in which the habit originates, then having that bad self pull (via the string) the bad thing away.

"It's a bit crazy," I said. "Where does the bad self go?"

"Just away from you. Just walking away."

"How is that healthy to watch a part of yourself walk away?"

"It's the unhealthy part of yourself. Dr. Michael is very interested in the many parts of a person."

"Yes, but aren't you supposed to integrate them? So you're not Sybil?"

"No, that's passé. That's, like, 1986. The new thinking is that you're supposed to just let the bad parts of yourself go, leave. Don't try to understand or dissect, just dismiss."

The waitress brought me a big plate of cottage-cheese pierogies, which sound gross but are the perfect food. Cuviendos smelled of garlic and new bread and some other basily, forest smell—the woodlands around Transylvania maybe! We had already drunk a carafe of wine between us. I tried to consult myself: Did I feel like many selves struggling or one whole, balanced self? What did it feel like to be alive? There is no answer for this or I would give it. But like everybody, I have moments when I lift my head and see a face as familiar as Bonnie-Beth's, like a clearing in a thicket, and somebody hands me a plate of Old World comfort food, and the night outside is black and starry, and the music inside rises, an old, somewhat sentimental and fascist violin, and if a person could describe everything—everything on the walls, the red velvet, the photos of the dead, and everything on the street outside, the thrilling carnival of the Village, Soho, and Chinatown and the Battery beyond spiraling down into darkness and the sea—if somehow you could get those details down, that would explain what it felt like to be a person alive, inside and warm, allowed to sit in the midst of it.

"He also advises sending letters to yourself, with advice and encouragement. I've done it; it really works. Especially if you make the letter from a version of yourself five years hence."

"How do you get over the embarrassment factor of doing such a thing, mailing yourself a letter, spending the twenty-nine cents?"

"You get embarrassed just by yourself, without witnesses?"

"Yes. Don't you? I thought everyone did."

"No, I don't. I guess it's just you!" She smiled. "Also, Dr. Michael had me write a letter to myself five years in the future, and he promises to send it to me then."

"I would hate to think of what my younger self would think of me now."

"I know. I was such an anorexic."

"Me too, though sort of a failed one. My letter would have been just admonishments to myself not to get fat."

"I know. I would be so disappointed in myself now."

Bonnie-Beth walked me up through the Village. We stopped at a table outside a shop where they were selling hats. I found shopping very upsetting, but Bonnie-Beth loved to do it. She put a hat on my head—a bowler. I looked in the little mirror that was set up on the table. "You look very Eastern European, very Milan Kundera." Bonnie-Beth was always ready to make fun affectionately of everybody, and in that you could feel her regard for you. "Perfect for your lovah in the park."

15

I was there before Peter, naturally. He was always late. By eleven-thirty I spotted him walking underneath the great Stanford White arch. Peter was carrying a small, white bag with hot bread in it. We sat for a while on the fountain as he tore off pieces of the bread for me. He seemed very merry tonight; I could see the lights of Fifth Avenue strung across his eyes like the lights along bridges. The longer we sat there, the less I was interested in going for drinks and telling him anything about work, about the dam, or the Noodle House. Washington Square is so self-contained and beautiful, and more than any other place in the city, it seemed to me completely unchanged from the 1970s when I would walk through it with my father on our way from church to the bakeries on Bleecker.

It did cross my mind to tell Peter something intimate, something non-work-related, to see where that got us. Instead we talked about the movie he saw, *The Crying Game*, which led into a discussion of the IRA, toward whom Peter

was deeply sympathetic, probably because they were the un-
derdog. Though he could also career around and express
sympathy suddenly for some of the worst tyrants in history—Mussolini, say, or Rasputin, or even Mao at times,
which was surprising given what had happened to Su Chen
in China. Peter seemed to feel about figures in history that
they were characters from a novel; the best ones were outsize, and what made them great was beyond morality. So no,
I never made a confession of love that night. In fact, I left
shortly after we met. Sometimes when I think back on the
series of mistakes I made from that moment on, it occurs to
me that perhaps this one was the gravest, never once to have
told Peter how I felt.

When I returned to my apartment that night, there was a
message from my mother, telling me that she had dropped off
a seafood terrine in my refrigerator and also that Francis had
called for my number. Then there was indeed a message from
Francis: "Dolly, I think I can help you. I've learned of another
spot near your little project, and I can help you acquire it. Can
you come see me?"

I found the terrine, which was one of my mother's special-
ties, a dish that captured in itself the brutality of life—all sorts
of gorgeous and strange sea creatures cheerfully brought together in her kitchen to be beaten, emulsified, heated, and
rolled into a log. I pulled out my futon that doubled as my
bed and turned on the television to watch the news.

This was an interesting offer, but I knew for sure Peter would refuse it. His hatred for Francis was pretty much implacable, and I knew Peter well enough to know that accepting a favor from Francis would be worse than letting the whole thing go down the drain. Still, how could I refuse? And anyway, why did I have to refuse? I felt suddenly angry at Peter. It was pretty much impossible to carry out his wishes, and if I had to resort to means he didn't understand or like, so be it.

Right as I was about to fall asleep, the phone rang: James. The studio was tightening the screws on him again. They hated each draft of his script more and more, and meanwhile, the shoot was set to begin in two weeks. "They want it to be more about the people," he said.

"Stupid movies about people," I said.

"They think I'm overly focused on this field of wheat where it's set."

"I thought it was about a superhero who turns from a man to woman."

"Right, but the thing that she's ultimately trying to protect is this field of wheat that has been genetically altered."

"Ah, altered to do what?"

"Increase confidence."

"You're kidding?"

"No, I'm not kidding."

"Oh."

"So the field is the main thing. The rest is secondary."

It did sound a bit boring. "Well," I said, "it must be wonderful to be shooting it back at home. It must be wonderful to have a home that you can always return to."

"I guess. Well, you have that. Your childhood home is still intact. Same thing."

"Yes, but it's an apartment. It's not land. Come to think of it, it's strange to have a family homestead hundreds of feet in the air. It's not natural."

"When I was young it seemed almost unbearably interesting to me that people lived in New York City in apartments and rode in a subway underground."

"You thought about us?"

"Yes. Did you think about me?"

"No."

"Of course."

"No, that's not true, I did. I thought of you out there under the stars, hoeing the wheat."

"Well, you don't really hoe wheat exactly. Nor would you do it under the stars."

"Well, whatever you did up there."

"Yeah," he said. "Whatever."

"I'm lucky you don't have a girlfriend," I said. "Otherwise I couldn't talk to you late at night."

"I do have a girlfriend."

"You're kidding."

"No."

"What's her name?"

"Charley."

"Is she a man?"

"No."

"What does she do?" This new information was very disturbing to me. "And you should mention her more, by the way."

"She's a speaker."

"What do you mean, a speaker?"

"For women's groups and such."

"What?"

"Like, a motivational speaker."

"You're dating a motivational speaker?"

"Yes."

"Oh dear," I said.

"I know," he said.

16

～

We met Peter right before the reading started; he was already seated in the NYU auditorium. Bonnie-Beth was so organized that she had brought an assortment of candies, all in threes so that she could share with Peter and me. "Bonnie, it's not a movie," I said. "It's a reading. It's like a lecture."

"Fine," she said and handed my Hershey's bar to Peter, so that he had two.

"I still want it," I said and took it back. For the rest of the lecture, Bonnie-Beth doled out candy very quietly and at regular intervals. It was like being with a really great mom all the time.

I did not necessarily expect it, but the book was beautifully written. Every line seemed inscribed with the tenderness Zhou felt for these two men, dreaming of heaven while living under the repressive, cruel regime of the emperors late in the eighth century. I could feel also a real sadness in the writing for China itself. Zhou's father had been a wealthy landlord before the Revolution and had been made to suffer horrendously for his wealth when Mao came along. Zhou, as a young Communist revolutionary, had even for a time turned against his own father.

Sometimes I wonder how it is that people who have money (my own family included) can relax at night. It can be taken away, everything can be redistributed in a heartbeat. There are always bands of revolutionaries forming in the hills, waiting. In China, in the early seventies, for instance, one day wealthy people felt perfectly secure and entitled and the next day they were terrified. Not only were their possessions and homes taken away, they were made to stand trial in struggle sessions for what they'd accumulated or inherited, and made to wear dunce caps or signs around their necks that said "Traitor to the People," or "Capitalist Running Dog." And they were killed. Or they were beaten, or sent north to labor camps, to die more slowly.

We cheered for Zhou when he came into the lobby after the reading. Bonnie-Beth had him sign about fifteen books that she'd bought for various relatives, and then we all retired to Sun Lok Kee for a late-night feast—green onion, sake, dumplings, and coconut good-fortune cake.

When I got home, there was another message from Francis on my machine: "Did you get my message? I've secured you a location. The way is clear. Call me, Dolly."

17

It's a bit of a grim parlor game among expats who were in China during the Revolution to speculate over who became disenchanted with Mao first. Everybody of course wants to have discerned it early, that Mao's ideas were destroying rather than saving the worker and the peasant. Interestingly, it was the Christians who first spoke out against him. This was not perspicacity necessarily, but likely a response to Mao's vehement hatred of all religion, particularly Christianity and Confucianism. He once said he would use Marx if he could as an axe to chop off the heads of his godly countrymen.

So it's not surprising that Francis Efferveti was one of the first people to stick his neck out regarding Mao. Even years later, he would bring it up a lot in conversation, the times when he risked his life to oppose Mao. And when the subject didn't come up naturally, he would suggest it by referring to other dead martyrs—Bishop Romero, who was killed by a sharpshooter in 1980 ("If they kill me, I will be resurrected in the Salvadoran people"), or Jacques Bunel, intrepid and gentle hero of Mauthausen. On this day in October in his office, Francis actually used the phrase "other dead martyrs," never mind the fact that he actually wasn't himself dead and was sitting right here in the UN building, looking out over a breezy fall day in Manhattan.

Francis was offering to help. There was a map of the world that covered nearly an entire wall, studded with thumbtacks at the places where he was carrying on his projects, crowded mostly in Asia. Soon there would be another one stuck there, along the Yangtze.

18

I let Peter choose the restaurant; his sensibility restaurant-wise was very much toward the down-and-out. He liked shabby little places that nobody knew about except him and the most hardscrabble of locals. Peter would talk about certain meals with such nostalgia—a tough, salty piece of reindeer jerky he'd eaten in a small Laplander shack, or a perfect piece of whitefish he'd bought from a stoned Swedish woman who'd soaked it in lye in the back of her van on Venice Beach. This was Peter's idea of a meal; you knew the person who made it and could discern something of who they were and where they were from in the food. At any rate, I agreed to go with him to Bill's, a grungy little place where supposedly Walt Whitman had written his Brooklyn Ferry poem. Of course, every place within a stone's throw of the Brooklyn Bridge tries to claim the poem was written there, a number rivaled only by the number of places around Jerusalem where the tree for the Cross was supposed to have grown and once blossomed.

Just as you feel when you look on the river and sky, so I felt. I could remember this much of the poem, which I had once known quite well. In fact, it made me think of James, since he and I had been such avid readers of poetry. In those days we were still very sensitive to language: I remember that a single phrase could interest me so completely that I would take it as my personal motto for days at a time. *Wake to your mermaid life!* Or, *Shall our blood fail? Or shall it come to be the blood of paradise?*

As a child, I had spoken Mandarin, which is not only a language but a way of seeing the world according to characters—not in increments but all at once, or at least as all at once as a mind can bear. When I first began to read poetry, particularly what were called "deep image" poems, it seemed quite similar to me, and when the right accumulation of images reached my brain and sounded its chord, there was a moment of pleasure that was like a drug to me. To this day, I'll be walking someplace beautiful, down to the Battery maybe, or up along the park, along its bright southern edge, and a flock of birds will soar suddenly up the street, and the breeze will lift so that the leaves tear themselves free from the trees. The moon will be waiting in the sky, beyond the green, spooky minaret of the Sherry-Netherland, though it's still a bright, sunny afternoon, and the bodies will be strolling or dodging the cars as they cross the street, and everybody will seem so high and resilient, and nature will appear to be at one with the city, and there will come to me an overwhelming, nearly frightening feeling for the beauty of life, its interlocking compounds of images, its sights piled one on top of another, and my mind will come to a sort of attention, to an ordering of all these images into sense and stillness, and then I'll realize that this is Mandarin, returned to me. Its inventors were the Mings, who were a brutal but happy people who presided over the beginning of the modern world, and who attempted to create a language system made up of characters who could each carry as much of the burden of the world as possible on their little backs, and thus revealed for us all a language as intricate and joyful and expressive as the living world.

Bill's was everything I thought it would be, and more: dark, reddish wood from floor to ceiling, the smell of the deep, rotting sea everywhere, and every surface—the floor, the counters, the walls, the tabletops—all managing, somehow, to be both dusty and covered with an almost imperceptible gelatinous film, a substance like jellyfish, or sea blubber.

Right after our meal was placed on the table, I looked up at Peter and told him. "The Noodle House has moved itself down the Yangtze." Peter had just dragged a squid out of his bowl. He had ordered squid ensance, which is basically steamed squid with pepper and salt. He sat there staring at me, his fork hovering in front of him, with the squid sitting on it, perched there, waiting, a little tiny octopus. It looked really disturbing; in fact, I think it's in general gross to eat whole animals that have larger versions of themselves in the world somewhere. Like having a tiny pony standing on your fork and then eating it. And there *were* squid up to one hundred feet long floating—menacing and languid—in the depths of the ocean. On the table the waiter had also placed some French fries, and some glistening sautéed carrots, and also already our desserts, two large pieces of frosted rum cake, which I for one hadn't eaten since I had a British nanny back in middle school. The food was not really that good, but it was suggestive.

I repeated myself. "The Noodle House has moved itself down the coast." I pictured it going, carefully, on its stilts, its daddy-long-legs moving delicately up and down.

"What are you talking about?"

"The dimensions of the dam have been increased slightly, and it was enough to take out our land. I've found a place farther down the Yangtze. In some ways, it's a better location. I'll have the land surveys for you tomorrow."

"Why don't I know about this?"

"I'm telling you now," I said.

Peter's eyes revealed nothing for a moment. They were a sea blue and had grown paler every year from the diabetes. It's interesting that eyes can look so peaceful even as they labor endlessly, dividing the light, sorting through it the variations of shadow for a vision, flipping it right side up, again and again.

19

I was curious: James had given me a copy of the script and it was tucked away inside my coat as I walked home through the rainy streets. It was a warm but wet fall night, and the lights were blurring, and falling, pouring all around me. I kept catching little pieces of conversation as I walked through the Village crowds—*I should have been a food critic for the* New York Times *or the* LA Times, one man shouted from under his umbrella to his friend as I passed.

Once home, I made a gingerbread sheet cake for Bonnie-Beth's grandmother, who lived in a fancy, gold-plated suite in the Sherry-Netherland and was turning eighty tomorrow. While it baked—the smell suddenly suggesting a corner bakery that used to exist in the 1970s in Midtown—I listened to a photojournalist on *Fresh Air* talking about her various lovers in various war zones; she was very strenuous on the point that men at war are very good boyfriends as they are at last vulnerable and don't take you for granted and are always talking about their feelings. Something in the photojournalist's voice made me think she was making it all up, fantasizing. Anyway, even if it were true, how was it useful? We couldn't all go to the war zones.

After a few phone calls—my mother, Bonnie-Beth, one last check-in with James—I got into bed with the script. HARVEST, it said in block letters on the first page. "Story by James Nutter, script by James Nutter." It began with a long shot of a golden wheat field at harvesttime, the camera drawing closer and closer (*inclining* was the word James used) to reveal a boy running along one of the lanes of wheat toward home. The camera moved closer until we could see the boy's face—anguished and crying. He tripped, fell aside, out of the view of the camera, and then there appeared a few seconds later a girl of the same age, the same tearful look on her face, running again toward the farmhouse.

It was a very beautiful, plain-hearted script, despite its fantastical premise. I had visited James's farm years ago, when he'd returned home from college for his mother's funeral, so I could picture the script's field perfectly; it had appeared to roll out from the sliding-glass windows off their kitchen, long rows of durum wheat that were so perfectly straight it seemed one could look down their yellow, bristling alleys for miles.

I had a city person's stereotypes of that life. It was hard for me to believe people had grown up there—like growing up in paradise, a simple and plain paradise where you wake up every morning to a silence so deep it seems like foreboding, and to mist flying across the fields, a morning walk to pick up the mail, a breakfast of eggs and toast, a day of physical labor, a big roast beef and Jell-O salad and green beans, a visit from the neighbors, a game of pinochle or hearts, and then a long reading session under the slanted eaves of the bedroom, a kiss from your mother or father before sleep, *you my child in whom I am well pleased!*

The funeral was very beautiful and sad. His mother had been by all accounts an exceptional and loving woman. There were pictures of her all over the house, posing with her husband or with James, or with James's older brother, Bramichari, whose real name was William and who still lived at home. James was never able to tell me where that name Bramichari had come from—a cousin, maybe, he thought, back in the day. But it seemed to capture Bram perfectly—his stolidness and otherworldliness both, his lack of interest in social interaction, which seemed at times like a kind of enlightenment. He had an incredible intellect, though it tended to pool in very specific areas—English royalty, for instance, or trains and carriages from the early part of the century. In pictures, he was a little bear cub in his mother's arms. During the weekend of her funeral, Bram's sadness was the hardest to measure, since he showed and basically seemed to feel so little emotion, but he did appear distracted, as if there were sounding within him something unfathomable but real, like those great gongs from the church bells that came pouring across the fields—fulsome, reverberating, final.

Apparently, in her last days, she had called James in and asked him if Bram would be okay, even after their father died someday. James had said yes. She got what she needed, that last yes, and her spirit fled.

20

~

This crowded and ragtag corner of the East Village at twilight brought to mind nothing so much as Dante's first circle of hell, limbo, reserved for those souls who while on earth did not esteem virtue so much as life itself. I saw Peter crossing the street toward me, wearing a silvery gray suit that echoed the full moon beyond him. We walked the four blocks to the party, held in a three-story brownstone. People were sprawled elegantly and informally up and down the stairs, extending even into the street. The party evoked something biblical, with enormous bowls of figs and olives, and a silent agreement among many of the women that they wear sheathlike garments and hammered-metal jewelry. The minute Peter and I walked in I knew that this would be a good party for us. It was a book party, actually, but a fancy book, one that had already sold to the movies so that the party was making a trajectory into actual money. Somehow the combination of book and movie people always gave way to huge donations for Aquinas. Some parties Peter and I would walk into and realize instantly they were no good donation-wise. You could sense it right away, those rooms into which money flows and there reaches a standstill. Vases would be sitting there worth thousands of dollars. There was nothing more despairing, I'd come to believe after years with a charity, than to see a very expensive vase. What could you say about somebody who wanted to tie up tens of thousands of their dollars in a vase? It wasn't the amount that was the problem necessarily, just the stillness, the black-hole quality of it.

But here you could feel money moving through the room—invisible but palpable, rollicking about, changing hands. Here we would find people who didn't give to charity but only because it hadn't occurred to them. Peter would walk through the crowd, laying hands on their shoulders. He moved away from me as soon as we walked in, as was usual, which left me vulnerable to Christopher, who apparently had not yet departed for Rwanda. He approached me immediately, striding across the room. I managed to slip in a Xanax, which I was on the verge of taking anyway, and had become absolutely necessary with Christopher bearing down on me. "So you're going ahead with it?" he asked.

He was so tall he hovered over me. Christopher was from London originally, a tall Londoner who had spent years as a heroin addict and now was a macrobiotic health-food fanatic. This combination—tall and reedy and formerly

strung out but now brimming with health—was a gruesome one. His head itself was very tall and long, and it
swung precariously above me like a hanging lantern.

"Going ahead with what?" I asked.

"Your China project."

"We are," I said.

"Just like that?"

"Just like that, yes." I reached to the table behind me and
grabbed a shish kebab—some sort of mixed-meats extrava-
ganza, studded with onions.

"The Yangtze is the dirtiest river in the world."

"All the more reason."

"Erecting a hospital there is like erecting one on the op-
posite side of the Styx."

"It's not a hospital."

"This is just like Peter to crawl into bed with Deng Xiao-
ping."

"This is just like you."

"What?"

"To crawl in alongside them, nattering away."

"Do you know what will be the little bit of good you eke
out of this project?"

"What's that?"

"Your and Peter's salaries will be higher."

"That'll be a relief."

"The real reason Peter is involved in nonprofit work at

all is so that he can practice his architecture free from the desires of a client."

I couldn't really disagree with this, but I also didn't think it was a problem necessarily. That Peter had some personal investment in his work didn't cancel out its goodness. In fact, it seemed to me that people who were driven by some totally pure notion of goodness and charity were the most baffling people, in their way. Peter's motives were not selfless certainly, but it could be said his ambition intersected powerfully with the interests of others. "And Shelter the Children is so different?"

"I believe so."

"And why?"

"Because we happen to be collecting money for things that are needed in this world. Food and shelter. Baby formula. Remember, things like that?"

It was this sort of conversation that made me grateful to be working with Peter. However unnecessary his charity might be at least it was private. It was spun in a personal brain. Even if it was resulting in a strange pagoda to questionable end, teetering on the edge of the Yangtze. Anything was preferable to this generalized goodness that Christopher wanted to spread across the land. At any rate, I'd had this conversation a hundred times before. These parties, all parties, are full of charity people; I could point them out now, dotted through the crowd like secret agents. When they die they won't go to heaven, but rather to a terrace above heaven, where they can stand and talk about what can be done, what can we do, us mercy birds?

I heard Peter's laugh across the room, in the east corner. Peter rarely made jokes himself, but he had a talent for finding things funny, which is a special kind of intelligence. Somebody would say something in conversation and nobody would realize it was funny until Peter laughed, and then we'd realize it was the most hilarious thing. I looked toward him for a long while. His back was to me, and he was leaning forward to listen to a woman speak. I could see from here the black angles of his shoulder blades rising off his back as he inclined toward her. And for her part, she was beautiful. She appeared to be in her mid-forties, easily the best-looking woman in the room, and also the only one who had resorted to cleavage tonight.

I wondered what he was saying—a rundown of his life, possibly, if she'd asked—a childhood outside Memphis, Tennessee, then boarding schools, the books he'd loved as a child: Dickens, Defoe, Jack London, verging naturally into John Updike, Graham Greene, and William Styron when he was a teenager. Then college—Columbia—then divinity school, then China, then disenchantment with all things religious, then an MFA in architecture, and then China again and again, and Cambodia, and then Aquinas, and now the Noodle House. She would ask, I knew, why he'd named his charity Aquinas, and he would probably paraphrase Aquinas himself, who said that there are two aspects of intelligence: one is the curiosity to know whatever can be known, and the second is the ability to bear the understanding of where knowledge ends, beyond which one either perseveres with faith as into an unknown forest, or simply stands back in awe. And if this was happening, if he had said this to her, if he was already quoting Aquinas to her, and talking to her of what one does when confronting the unknown, the woman, her raven hair darkly absorbing the party's light, would be responding with the inner skepticism and attraction that I knew so well.

Christopher saw me looking at Peter, and he shook his head. "He's always up to something, isn't he?"

"You're an asshole, Christopher."

"You'll never give up, will you?" he said. And then, as an afterthought, "I'm an asshole? You think I'm an asshole. I'm not the one who treats you like this." He gestured toward Peter and the woman. Christopher spent as much time attacking Peter as stumping for himself, since he believed my feelings for Peter were what broke us up, rather than the obvious, which was Christopher's own terrible personality. I suddenly had a memory of Christopher undressed—everything about him disdainful of all things not righteous, everything not full of care—his arrogant mug, his long limbs, his body so reproachful and vaguely emaciated, as if he were in league with the starving. When I was involved with him, he was second in charge of public relations at Shelter the Children, and largely responsible for Shelter's controversial ad campaign wherein small children were shown naked and emaciated. In one photo used, which had won a Pulitzer for its photographer, there was a small boy, nearly dead, with a vulture flying overhead, its powerful wings full of life, floating there with a terrifying patience. "Care-porn," the *London Daily* called it. Though it was an undoctored photograph, you would still recoil from its use, at the sight of it, at its racial leveraging, at its ability to generate literally millions of dollars whose use was not quite clean, ever. The photo came to represent, for a time, what critics felt was a kind of smarminess on the part of charities, using such a painful image to get money. I knew this criticism well and could feel it myself; it was obvious. On the other hand, it was a real boy in the photo, and it was a real vulture, and on top of that, this was not the only boy or the only vulture, so it really was representative, and a person could never quite feel entirely comfortable blaming Christopher for pointing it out.

21

The morning was stormy and the Hudson River was rearing unnaturally on her shores, threatening to spill over. Peter was at his desk, his feet kicked up, reading the newspaper. He was eating oatmeal and had mixed in raspberries, so their scent was filling the office. I happened to be talking on the phone to Bonnie-Beth while I opened the morning's mail.

"Is the officious Peter in the room?" she asked.

"Officious?"

Peter lifted his head and looked at me. He knew this referred to him. Bonnie-Beth let it be known occasionally that she didn't really like him. I often tried to chalk this up to the fact that he was not as in love with me as we all hoped for, but maybe it was also because she'd spotted something in Peter that I, with my still-child's eyes in reference to him, couldn't always see. Occasionally I would get a hint of it— his weirdness, his chill, his sort of snobbery, his sense of homelessness in the world that he unconsciously brought on himself because of his contempt for what he called the "settled class," whoever that was—happy people, maybe, or people who lived in as he called it the bosom of the community, or in stable domestic arrangements, or just anybody who didn't spend their lives moving restlessly around the world searching for a home. But then my attraction always kicked in. Ultimately, I saw Peter as Su Chen had—tall gweilo, hair turning sandy in the summertime and falling in waves across the forehead, carrying inside himself the power to remake almost any situation, surrounded by yellow light of confidence, red light of love, a brilliant, independent mind. Brave!

"Why?" I said. And then Bonnie-Beth commenced with her lecture regarding the futility of finding love with Peter. In the midst of it, which I'd heard nine million times before, I came across a letter from the novelist I had seen on the stand at Mr. Burns's trial. His name was David League, and he had written this letter by hand, in tall, sinister, and prissy handwriting, like a note from an old great-aunt.

"I gotta go," I said to Bonnie-Beth.

"Fine, fine," she said. "Call me back." I had already started to read the terrifying letter, which was sending through me waves of panic—which as they rose through me totally obliterated my little shares of well-being, shares that I was always surprised to find out were based on rows of numbers adding sensibly in relation to other rows of numbers, all of which made possible the future, including Peter's outsize plans, and my feeling that I was making his life as he wanted it possible, which in the romantic confusion in my brain I thought would make him love me.

"Oh no," I said as I scanned the letter further. Somehow my letter supporting Mr. Burns had fallen into the hands of this David League. After a few token remarks of praise for all our hard work at the Aquinas Foundation, he described himself as the head of something called the Artists' Alliance, an organization formed to defend artists against "the excesses and abuses of those bottom-line mongerers who would profit off their artistic and creative natures." The letter went on to request that Aquinas return to the artists all the money they had given to Mr. Burns and which in turn he had donated to Aquinas.

"What, what?" Peter kept saying, so I took it to him. And then, "Oh my, are we the bottom-line mongerers?" Finally he looked up at me. "Is this something we need to worry about?"

"I would say possibly. He threatens to report it to the *Times*."

"Would the *Times* really care that a bunch of artists got duped?"

"Possibly."

"What would it do to us to excise that money from our operations?"

"We couldn't excise it, more like skim it."

"Well, let's then."

Let's then. As always, my job seemed very simple to Peter. But that's how I spent the rest of the day—extracting from the many-headed river running through our office a settlement. It's not of course easy to separate money from money. People donate money for this or for that, and then types of money bond together and cannot be separated, one from another. And then the money itself seems to exert its many personalities—shrinking or expanding according to some emotional formula I could not always crack. But one thing I had was faith that one could, if you used one hand in judgment and the other in love, confer on a budget a kind of power and confidence. As with something from nature, you could help it to grow. And anyway, this was all I had for Peter, this little rearranging I could do, into the night. I could make a place for Peter to practice his strange and maybe compromised charity. I could make a *dwelling in the evening air,* for the two of us.

22

Eventually that day, with the assistance of one Xanax and two Advil Cold & Sinuses, which together create the perfect emotional equilibrium of peace plus energy, I managed to settle in my mind and in the books an amount Aquinas would be willing to give back to the so-called victims of Mr. Burns. It wasn't all the money we'd received from Mr. Burns, but it was in the hundreds of thousands, which was a deep, irreversible sacrifice for us. We needed to do it, however, so as not to risk public exposure as threatened by the hippies of the Artists' Alliance.

By evening I'd basically located all the money, just in time to slip out with Peter for a nice quiet dinner with some friends of his, the Tetreses. We met them at Prima, in Brooklyn, near Peter's place. The Tetreses—Bill and Nancy—had married young and now had been married for twelve years. They were both engineers, specializing in water distribution, particularly filtering and cleaning water as it came into living environments.

It had become clear to me that the Tetreses were working out some marital problems in the plumbing and water redistribution plans they were drawing up for the Noodle House. They were both brilliant engineers, but their marriage was so terrible and nevertheless so socked in and vital to them both that they couldn't help but express at every moment, with every gesture, how they felt about each other. In the relationship between the Tetreses, both genders seemed to find their worst expression—the unthinking cruelty of man, the longing for humiliation of woman—and yet in the right amounts, in the right equation, these two qualities can form a truly lasting, implacable bond, unfortunately.

We met them in front of the Promenade, then proceeded to Prima. As soon as we sat down, Mrs. Tetres started in. One thing I've not picked up, not having had a child, is the ability to talk about truly gross and bodily things as if they are cute somehow, little pieces of intimacy. Tonight Mrs. Tetres was telling us a story from early in the marriage that involved them burying the placenta that accompanied their third child, which then got dug up—a dried-up mass of interlocking veins—and carried into the house by their dog Cash. However badly I was taking this information, Peter was worse off, which he registered by having no expression whatsoever on his face. Mrs. Tetres was very pretty, very well put together, very much more womanly than I. There was some essential womanliness to her that made me feel like whereas she was bursting forth, I was always pulling back, emotionally, like a man. She kept dragging me away from the main conversation, which actually happened to be quite interesting as Peter and Mr. Tetres were both political junkies, into tinier discussions between the two of us. She would ask me things under her breath, as if women were meant to murmur back and forth while the men truly talked. Probably if she had had her way, as the men talked about the world and its great events, she and I would have clasped hands, pledged friendship and love.

In return for their work on the Noodle House, Peter was designing the plans for a house they were building in Roxbury, Connecticut. It came out later in the evening that the Tetreses were going to go out to this land before anything was built on it and just try to live there, without even a tent, and see how it was that they lived, and then they wanted to build a house around their needs as their needs naturally expressed themselves one by one. For instance, they would see in which direction they naturally slept, and then where in proximity to where they slept would they go to prepare the food rations they'd brought, and so on. And they wanted Peter (and me) to come watch them live and then sketch the plans for the house accordingly.

"So," I said, "at the beginning, there'll just be the field and you two."

"Yes," said Mrs. Tetres. "We'll just go out to the field, on a Friday afternoon, say, and we'll just crouch down there and start living, and Peter can begin his drafting."

It was the worst thing I'd ever heard. I thought this was a good time to exercise my right and even duty to step in and head off people who wanted too much of Peter's time. "I just don't think we have the time," I said.

"I think we can do it," Peter said.

"Really? You have your class at the New School, and the Noodle House plans have got to be complete by next month."

"I think this is worth it. Do you know that Reed College in Oregon was built this way? Christopher Alexander designed it by letting children play in the snow, and then in the summer, he put gravel paths where they ran, and placed buildings at the locations where they huddled to talk."

"Fine," I said, turning to the Tetreses. "We'll be ready."

"And we shall be the children," Mrs. Tetres said, her eyes glistening as she looked up at her husband, "playing in the snow."

23

James's favorite restaurant was on Sixth Street, named Kismoth. We were there on a cool October night. Our waitress, who was also the owner, knew James very well because James had dated her daughter, briefly, at Harvard. The daughter had broken up with him shortly before I met him, but her name—Serena Katsabrahmanian, shortened to Kat—had still hovered over our friendship. Her mother, our waitress, had once been Miss Bombay, and she appeared to love James. "My favorite one," she said and set down some very beautiful condiments with our pappadums, little swirling sauces with twigs and pebbles strewn across them.

"Look at this," James said to me as soon as we'd ordered, and slid a shiny piece of paper—a fax—across the table. It was from the movie studio, signed by an executive named Michael English. It read:

Dear James:
As you say, the plains are indeed a humble beauty, but

on the other hand, even you would have to admit that it's a bit boring to watch wheat grow. Unfortunately it's not on anybody's mind when they attend a movie what wheat looks like under the earth, however much it should be! Would that we were producing a documentary about prairie grasses: your script would be perfect. The most attractive option to us at this point, I'm afraid to say, is to pass on your script to somebody less enamored of wheat fields and get on with making an evocative, interesting action movie, as was our intent.

"Would they do that? Pass on your script to somebody else?"

"Yes," he said, drumming his fingers on the table. "Let me ask you: Do you think it's interesting that some sheaves of wheat don't make it out of the ground, that the strongest can shoot up too quickly and actually break on the ceiling of the earth?"

"Do I find that interesting?"

"Do you find that interesting?"

"Only somewhat."

"What if I could show it to you visually, on the screen?"

"That doesn't sound that interesting to me."

"It is interesting. It's quite interesting."

"I think it says good things about you that you find it interesting."

"I know they'd like it if I could just get some of it down on film. If they would give me just a bit of freedom. But they're actually sending this guy up to Saskatchewan to babysit me during the shoot."

Kat's mother brought us our food—aloo saag (potatoes and spinach) for me, and lamb for James. "I'm going to try to forget about this," he said. "I think they're just trying to scare me. Anyway, this weekend is going to be great. I've got a lot of things planned for us." For a minute I thought he meant him and me, but then he said, "Touristy-type things. Statue of Liberty, Empire State, Tavern on the Green."

"Is Bram coming this weekend?" Bram had come for yearly visits when James was in college, and they'd kept up the tradition. I very much looked forward to seeing Bram again; he was so interesting—removed, formal, polite, old-fashioned. It was somewhat difficult for him to travel, but as long as things adhered to a schedule, he was okay. The most offensive thing to him was spontaneity.

"Bram is coming after we shoot the movie. This weekend Charley is coming. I didn't tell you? Charley."

My heart sank a little. Charley: short for Charlemagne. His girlfriend—fledgling actress and motivational speaker. She was the lucky one, I thought. The city was in general better with James in it—things seemed more intense and also happier. After dinner we set out into the autumn evening, leaves everywhere underfoot. Every storefront and restaurant seemed to be alive with warmth, and people were feeling again what a revelation the city was, all those beautiful rooms carved everywhere into the stone, all the lovely, strange interiors, all the homes, even the plainest room a treasure against the encroaching cold.

Down Broadway I saw a policeman pass by on a horse, the horse's mane dividing New York into west and east. Perhaps because I was with James, fragments of a Stevens line flew through my mind—*winter and summer embrace and forth the particulars of rapture come.* But please! Here I was, imagining James and me as a couple. It was silly. It was really just myself as a younger, more idealistic person that was making me nostalgic. At the time, being twenty years old was actually sort of laborious, but in retrospect I couldn't help but see it as a very raucous, liberated time, when I was at one with everything good—the outdoors, poetry, my outraged sense of justice. I had once talked James into living in a little shanty on the campus green to protest the school's investments in then still-apartheid South Africa. It had been springtime, our junior year, and we had stayed up late every night, reading and studying by kerosene lamp. I came to love returning home to James in our little cardboard fort every night. In those days the deepest relationships were platonic, and to sleep with somebody was to make him temporary, and to take him outside the realm of intimacy. So James and I were true companions, inseparable.

Anyway, his actress girlfriend was coming to town, so why was I going on like this, what was my problem?

24

The next afternoon as Peter left to teach his class, I went to the courthouse to offer back the money to the Artists' Alliance. I thought I'd catch up with David League after court let out for the day and hand over the money.

When I arrived, Mr. Burns was still in his last hours on the stand, spending his light extravagantly. He seemed to be airing all his guilt in court, for everything he'd done in his life, the sort of guilt—elusive as original sin—that wasn't useful at all to Leonard Keen. Mr. Burns was telling an elaborate gothic tale of a debutante who'd died in 1958, and whom he'd later dug up and whose heart he heroically cut out in order to discern in the moonlight if she'd been poisoned. The story was of course an insane fiction but the court was nevertheless letting him tell it, via something his lawyers called "requisite revelation." On these grounds, they let him elaborate endlessly, as if by letting Mr. Burns garrulously admit to all these grotesqueries, they could somehow impress the court with the fantastical nature of his mind and also obscure the specific act of fraud in question inside a more general account of mismanagement, suggesting that Mr. Burns also lost his own considerable fortune assiduously and foolishly. If a man squanders his own money, the reasoning went, can you really blame him for squandering somebody else's money? Then it would be not fraud, just incompetence. I actually didn't know myself where I stood on the question of Mr. Burns's culpability. Sometimes he would look at me with a kind of intense, intelligent eye, making its way suddenly through the genial, blustery, old southern dandy façade, and I would see that he was putting one over on all of us all of the time. But then it would pass, and his true self—vulnerable, overwrought, and completely irrational—would return.

I caught up with David League and the lawyer Keen in the hallway, as they were striding toward the front doors at the end of the day. I stepped in front of them. "My name is Justine Laxness. I'm with Aquinas."

"Oh," David League said. He stopped walking just as we stepped outside the building, into a dark draping itself all over the city. Some doves skittered away from the steps, toward the river. "The woman with the money," he said. Leonard Keen said nothing. There was something birdy about him up close; he had that sharp, impersonal look birds have.

"How was the day today?" I said, gesturing toward the courtroom.

"It was excruciating, as usual," David League said.

"Really?"

"Your Mr. Burns can be a real manipulator."

"He can be."

"Your efforts to present him as crazy are disgusting to me."

"My efforts?"

"Yours or your organization's. Whomever's. I don't make distinctions between corporations and the people who run them," David League said. Keen smoothed his hand over his ponytail, as if he wore it as a symbol of this philosophy.

"You're making an assumption not based on evidence," I said, sort of a little lawyer joke, but they didn't observe it.

"And what's that?"

"That I conspired to get his money. Mr. Burns simply donated this money to us."

"So you're saying you won't be returning this money to the victims."

"I didn't say that," I said, and this annoyed him.

"Look, I'm very busy," he said. "I don't have time to have conversations with the mistress of such a sketchy organization unless you have something to tell me—a confession, an admission, a written promise."

I was planning on giving David League the money then, and there was a momentary distraction, a shadow that passed between us and the setting sun. We all turned to see a man opening his coat toward us, to show us rows and rows of condoms, pinned to the lining, each for a dollar. The seller lifted his eyebrows. It was all deeply embarrassing, this suggestion of sex between us. Keen vigorously shook his head no, his ponytail wagging. But in the time it took for this to transpire, the words "written promise" kept running through my mind. It occurred to me that they might want a written promise so that he could use it in the trial against Mr. Burns as proof that we knew the money had been illegally acquired. And though I was willing to give back some of the money we'd received from Mr. Burns, I was not necessarily anxious to betray him and to jeopardize Aquinas's continued relationship with his wealth.

I felt more courageous now that I saw they possibly had their own little agenda running through the proceedings.

"Look," I said. "We're planning on giving back a sizable portion of Mr. Burns's donation, but it will take time."

"And why's that?" David League asked.

"Well, it will take time to retrieve the money from its other projects."

"How much time are we talking about?"

"A few months."

"This is not your decision. This is money you've stolen."

"I did not steal this money, nor did my partner. We have no legal responsibility to return it."

"No, of course not. This is exactly why people launder

money, to pass it into hands that are seemingly cleaner and cleaner, to give the appearance of ethical cleansing." David League looked so mild—brown corduroys, sandals, feathered hair—that to hear him talk like this was truly dispiriting.

"We were not at all aware this was happening."

"The degree of your ignorance is not interesting to me," David League said. And then, at about exactly the wrong moment, Mr. Burns came to me, throwing open the great heavy doors, calling me "beloved," offering me both of his thick hands, with which he drew me into his fleshy embrace. When I emerged from the darkness, moments later, David League and Leonard Keen were already taking flight down the long stairs.

25

Later that day Peter and I were both back in the office, moving about—arranging, organizing, ruminating. Late in the day was our most intimate time together, according to me. Sometimes I would go out for a sandwich or takeout and bring it back for our dinner. As I'd be returning, approaching our building, I'd look up at our windows from the sidewalk and see them brimming with light as the day's radiance failed, and I would be so in love with that light, as other women are in love with the light that falls out of their home as they walk up a snowy lane toward it.

I hadn't gotten around to telling Peter what had transpired that day. I thought I would casually insert it into the conversation at some point, that I was waiting just a little while longer to give back the money to Keen and the artists. Instead, I had brought us some Chinese food, set it out between my desk and his drafting board. I was working on a grant application to submit to the Ford Foundation. It was definitely autumn by now, ribbons of cold running through our open windows. I passed over to Peter some of what we called "bagpipes," whose real name was bagh pih—a carton of cold, silver noodles and slivers of almond and duck breast. I noted once again that he was capable of eating with chopsticks while keeping his right hand free to sketch; tonight he was drawing a little room, a tidy, angled, overwrought room in the Noodle House that would never be, to commemorate his love for Su Chen. Suddenly I was just so frustrated with him, and myself, and the situation in general. It wasn't lovely, to live in the past. It was fruitless. And it wasn't just Peter's love that kept him facing Su Chen's grave, but it was his love mixed with guilt that made it so enduring.

I hoped there was a heaven, where she could forgive him and he could feel finally what he wanted the Noodle House to grant—forgiveness. Of course once this happened he would not return whole to me, but would enter eternity with Su Chen, as lovers do. A pigeon squawked outside the window, on our crumbling little porch. "You should just die," I said, very quietly. This surprised me. I don't know why I said it aloud, except that maybe it was a statement so perfectly balanced in my mind between cruelty and compassion that it slipped out like water at the moment it rises high enough to pass over a rock ledge.

"What?" he said.

I had tears in my eyes. I was horrified by how much I

loved him, and how much I wanted to hurt him. His hands were trembling, as always, a small, craggy piece of black charcoal in them.

"Nothing," I said. "I'm sorry."

I pulled on my coat and left then. "I'll see you later," I said. I called James from a pay phone and asked him to meet me in Chinatown, but when he paused and there was silence on the line, I remembered that Charley was in town this weekend.

"Oh," I said. "Hey, never mind."

"No, no," he said. "We'll both come. Just give us a half hour or so to get there."

I walked around Chinatown for a while, drank some green tea from a styrofoam cup, and took a Xanax. The leaves were falling on the bustling street; it was very pretty. And there were streamers of cold air running in a celebratory way through the fall night. Chinatown never failed to cheer me. I didn't think of it as reminiscent of China, or as an approximation, but as an actual piece of it that had made its way across the world and landed in NYC.

When I was a child, most of my playmates in China were Chinese, and I felt like a big blond monster. I can recall crying to Su Chen that I wanted to be Chinese. Su Chen couldn't bear it. You are, she'd say, bending down to my face. I can see her even now—braids swinging, chicken pox scars indenting her forehead, her olive skin, the subtle difference of her eyes, which I thought extremely pretty. She'd cover my heart with her hand. "Asia's in the heart!"

When James and Charley arrived at the corner of Grand and Mott, where we'd agreed to meet, they were red-cheeked, happy, alive in that way people newly in love are. Charley was quite intimidating. She was very self-confident, casual, cool. She was articulate and spirited, and she did yoga, so she seemed supremely comfortable in her own body, and also with silence, and for that matter with ambiguity. At dinner I could see that she did tend to veer into philosophical, somewhat New Agey territory, and I could see this made James uncomfortable. At one point she got on a tangent about immortality: what I remember most is that she said immortality is a guest in this mortal world, as our souls are guests in our mortal bodies.

I actually liked this kind of talk. Also, I was busy trying to imitate her posture, which, like all actresses', was exquisite. James changed the subject immediately.

"You seemed troubled on the phone," he said to me.

"I'm fine," I said.

"What was it?" Charley said.

"Oh just garden-variety sadness. I had a fight with my boss." I had been drinking too much, and that combined with the green tea and Xanax was making me feel my own pain perhaps a bit too garrulously. "But it's just, sometimes I look at my life and wonder, I mean, where's my family? Where are my children?"

"Well, you actually have to go ahead and have them," James said.

Charley looked at him disapprovingly. "It's healthy to long for things you don't have," she said. "It's what we're made for."

What a nice thing to say! She cast a very reasonable light on the human condition, just like that. After dinner we all three went walking. We passed a vendor selling, among other things, photos of Mao. Sometimes at these little shops they had kitschy Mao paraphernalia—key chains and bobble heads—but you could tell this seller was a believer. Mao looked kind and courageous in the photographs. After his death, the Chinese Council on the Revolution had made a finding that Mao had been seventy percent right and thirty percent wrong.

"When I was a child, I said a pledge every morning to Mao," I told them.

"What was it?" James asked.

"The sun in my heart is Mao Tse-tung. The sun in my heart is Mao Tse-tung. The sun at the heart of my dreams is Mao Tse-tung."

"Didn't your parents worry that you were learning to worship Mao?"

"Well, I don't know. I don't think they really knew the extent of it. But also, my mother is very tolerant. She believes in belief itself. She always wanted us to have hope, to believe in things. But she wasn't particularly doctrinaire about what we believed. It was the believing itself."

"Good missionary," James said.

This made us laugh. It was quite cold by now, and every store in Chinatown was brilliantly lit and inviting. We passed under the awning of Tim Yick, and I felt like ducking inside, into its healing cures and bins of roots, its suggestion that we could all be better if the right substance were found, shaved off the horn of a ram, or deep in the marrow of the yucca tree. The thought of my mother gave me peace. She had long ago, when I was a child, cleared away in my mind the ability to hope and to pray. She had always aspired herself after those almost mystically happy religious people— Bonhoeffer's implacable generosity and optimism on his last day in prison even as he knew he would die, Thomas Merton on his hill of joy, Simone Weil, Emerson, Bronson Alcott, even Milton and even Dante, who saved a ring of hell for those who despaired when they could have rejoiced. In fact, it was my mother who had introduced Peter to the thought of Aquinas, to the life concealed in Christ, and had given our charity its name.

By the end of the night, my feelings for Peter had returned to normal again, by which I mean they were back in limbo. Though my mother and Bonnie-Beth and, in truth, probably anybody who bothered to think about it at any length, regarded my waiting for Peter as a minor tragedy, I didn't mind it. I had become comfortable. I was now thirty-one and had pulled myself out of any number of stupid entanglements, and I think that part of why I maintained so easily my unrequited love for Peter was that it was oddly stable. After all, I saw him every day, and that fact alone could, for whole months at a time, put me under the illusion that my romantic life had reached some sort of clearing, say, a flax-gold field, where one's desires were never quenched but also never entirely awoken.

26

"I think we have to break up," James said the next time I saw him. We were at Kismoth again.

"But we're so happy!" I said.

He smiled briefly. "I feel terrible about this."

"Ah," I said. "How can you possibly break up with her? She's perfect. I love her."

"But all that stuff about immortality and the soul?"

"You like that."

"I hate it."

"You like it in literature."

"Not in conversation. To get a little lecture about it from your girlfriend just seems a little silly to me."

"It's just because she's beautiful."

"What?"

"Men don't want to hear anything philosophical from a pretty woman. It confuses them."

"I'll never be able to sleep with her again without imagining that she's thinking about immortality being in love with mortality, or some rubbish."

"You're squeamish. What is a woman supposed to think about while sleeping with you?"

He shrugged.

"A dial tone," I said.

"Isn't the woman supposed to be thinking about me?"

"Gross. That's just silly. Nobody wants that."

"I'm leaving in a week," he said after we'd eaten for a while. "You won't have me to kick around anymore."

"Up to Saskatchewan?"

"Yes. We have a three-week shoot, so I'll be there until Thanksgiving."

"So soon? Aren't you still disagreeing about the script?"

"Yes. It's getting worse. Michael English is now for sure coming along for the shoot. He'll be hovering over us the whole time, making sure we don't waste money doing anything even vaguely interesting."

"Maybe you're going to have to sneak out at night and shoot."

"After Michael English goes to sleep."

"How are you going to show the man turning into the woman?"

"Well, mostly that's off-screen, you know, he turns around and there she is. But also I do want to use the wheat as a visual metaphor for transformation."

In the most recent of Michael English's faxes, he had written, *objects, even objects in nature, can only carry so much of the weight of the film, and yet a person can carry a whole world of ideas and associations and plotlines, don't you see?*

Of course James had been raised on Rilke, and Bishop, and Stevens, for whom objects were as sturdy and reliable a vehicle as any person, if not more so. Despite the relative charm of Michael English's faxes, James had worked up a real scorn and hatred for him and had already instructed the entire crew in advance to not speak to him the whole shoot.

27

"The Tetreses have gone and done it," Peter said the minute I stepped into the office on Saturday.

"What?"

"They're in the field."

"You're kidding."

"The forecast was good, and they went, quite suddenly."

"So it's begun," I said.

"They want us as their guests tomorrow night."

"Oh no."

"Where we choose to lie shall be the guest room."

We took Peter's car, which he almost never used—a 1977 brown Mustang. The ride was up and out on the FDR, and then into the raw, beautiful fall of upstate New York and Connecticut. It was almost ridiculously beautiful. Why would the trees, in preparation for winter, have to be so colorful? There's of course ample reason why flowers need to be so lovely at the height of their fertility, but leaves need not go into such a brilliant sunset right before they fall and die.

Two hours outside the city, we found the Tetreses lying on their land. They were napping in the late-afternoon sun. We had picked up chow mein and its accoutrements in downtown Roxbury (an exquisite small town, by the way, where people assumed Peter and I were a married couple), and we carried it out to them. There was a tarp tented over them, on four sticks, to block out the sun and presumably any rains that came, and there already was a semblance of order among their things. The kitchen items were all grouped together—a coffeemaker and a little cooler, various snacks in baskets—and then their bedroom, where they now lay, was off a more central main area. But these areas were all still imaginary, essentially. Peter pretended to knock on a front door and then called out, *hello, hello.* I was just looking at them, thinking they were so strange to have fallen asleep out here in the meadow. They were curled together, though, which sort of put to shame all my insistence that they were the worst, most dysfunctional couple I knew, a thought that quickly reinstated itself however when we all sat down to eat together in the space that would become the dining room. We were talking of Peter's operation last winter for a hernia, a conversation that began because it took Peter about a hundred hours to get down on the ground. Mrs. Tetres patted the earth beside her for Mr. Tetres to sit down. He sat a little ways away, and she scooted over to get closer. "I like to scootch over close to him," she said, winking at me.

After dinner, Peter went walking with Mr. Tetres, so Mrs. Tetres and I had some coffee and settled down where the couches would be in the living room and began a deep conversation on the tiniest of Mrs. Tetres's preferences. "I'd like to put a couch here," she said, "because the picture window then will be back here." She pointed behind her head. "It won't be too bright in the day to read, but still plenty of light, and then at night, I'll have a lamp right here over my head, so I can read. And when I'm reading, I like to just pivot a bit"—she craned her neck—"and be able to look at the window. Especially at sunset, I'll be able to read, and then pivot my head, and see out the window. Because when I read, I don't want the window right there in front of me, because it's too distracting, but I also want to be able to gaze off when I've enjoyed a passage in the book and I want to pause just to soak it in."

I tried to peer through the gloaming and see if Peter and Mr. Tetres were coming back soon. But they were gone, over hill and dale. Once Mrs. Tetres had told Peter and me that whenever she spoke to children she crouched down so she was at eye level. "I crouch down," she had said, so Peter and I have often repeated it, in times when we needed to brag about some inconsequential thing, "I crouch down." I saw Peter then, coming across a black patch of lawn. He and Bill Tetres looked like miners returning home to us from a long day at work. I've never been particularly marriage-minded, but it's impossible not to notice that some women get men who return like this to them every night as the sun falls. They await the man in a big home, lit with lamps, filled with music and love.

"You know, this is a really beautiful piece of land," I said to Mrs. Tetres. There was actually heather in the dimming hills, purply and velvet.

"Thank you, Justine," she said. Her eyes were very pretty, very green, the lamplight falling across her face, darkness and light. "I hope you'll come often. We want the house full of people, full of children and happiness and animals."

Children and happiness and animals. I was just thinking it was the kind of insane thing she would say, sort of sweet but also somewhat ridiculous. There was a river that ran along the edge of the property, and its toads were suddenly coming awake. They sounded nearly mechanical, they were so loud and percussive. I peered down at the stream. I could still see the silver flashing ribbon in the dying light, rushing. On its other side were some pines and some elm trees, black silhouettes.

After a fire, Peter and I settled into our "bedroom." We lay back on the ground in our sleeping bags and stared up at the dark night, punctuated only by millions of tiny stars.

"I feel like the first man!" he said, a bit under his breath since the Tetreses were sleeping a few feet away.

"You're not," I said. "You're about the fourteen trillionth."

"I feel like the fourteen trillionth man!" he said.

It was a perfect night. I'd forgotten how liberating it feels to sleep in the open air. All around us there was a clamor of sound, the buzzing landscape, the *tick tock tick tock* of some strain of cricket, the late-night meadowlark. The Buddha said, *What if we had nothing? Then we would have everything.*

"Good night, Peter," I said.

"Good night, little one."

Which of course was a nearly insanely infantilizing thing to say and provided me with ample evidence once again that Peter was not romantically interested in me and never would be. Even as I turned thirty-two, he still wouldn't recognize me as anything except his friends' daughter. In fact, the distance in age between the Tetreses was at least as wide as the years between us, and look at them, just a few feet away, serene as they slept, sleep in its mercy pulling the plug on their personalities, their bodies fitted together snugly in the place where their bed would eventually be, under the window, into which the moon—beautiful, reliable—would shine every night.

28

October flew by. One minute we were inside the end of summer and the next hurtling toward winter. The Noodle House was growing, changing, under Peter's solicitude, and the Artists' Alliance had stopped breathing down my neck, the artists retreating back into their arts as animals into their cages, and for a few days, as New York City swirled around in a beautiful, cool, and sun-laden fall, it seemed that all was well, both in China and in New York City, a rare moment of equilibrium for me.

Except for the calls from James, up in Canada, where the movie was grinding to a halt. In fact, word had already leaked to *Variety* that the film was in trouble. I picked up a copy in Soho and read all about it one morning: after five days of filming, nearly a quarter of its budget had been spent and only two of its 133 pages had been shot. There was even a picture of James, and somehow the article and picture in combination made him out to be somewhat of a megalomaniac let loose on the prairies, there to catch the "idiom of the American heartland," which unfortunately was a direct quote from James, but it didn't capture his true nature and humility. In the picture his hair was in big, weather-beaten drifts in the wind.

I knew from our phone conversations that James was actually very worried. Some nights when I talked to him on the phone, he couldn't even catch his breath. I would just listen to him trying to breathe. I was so scared one night that I started crying on the phone, asking him to please speak. Finally, after just a week and a half of shooting, the worst came to pass and the studio pulled their money entirely, allowing James to finish the week's shots but no more while they looked for a new director to take over the material.

29

On the plane I read a Cassils book of Peter's that I had grabbed on my way out of the office. It was essentially a book about crowds, specifically a crowd's ability, or inability, to think ethically. Peter had underlined a great deal, and I found myself skipping from one underlined passage to the next. I realized as I read, the overhead light like a spotlight on Peter's selections—"a crowd is a beast and cannot think as a man"—that Peter must have been thinking at least a little about the Red Guards and the Cultural Revolution when he read it. It was impossible not to, though Cassils was writing at the turn of the century, when Mao was just a little boy running alongside the Wu Shan River in Hunan Province.

I fell to sleep and perhaps not surprisingly to a dream of Su Chen alive. When I woke we were making our descent into Saskatchewan, which felt to be already deep inside winter. Once we'd landed and I'd gotten my luggage, I stepped outside the terminal into a cold so terrible that it stopped my breath. The inside of the cab was such a relief—smoky, warm, somewhat dirty air. I felt so grateful for the heat that came out of that cab's vents, though it reached me as just slender filaments that could only remind me that one day I might be warm again. It was a dim, austere, late afternoon, and the city of Regina was beautiful and lonely at this time of day and year—solitary prairie city sunk in a cold, bright sunset.

The end of the city was abrupt, and we slipped into the darkening plains instantly, our wheels rolling along effortlessly. I nearly fell asleep again during the twenty minutes it took to get to the farm, and then was shocked at the great light that seemed to hover over the Nutter farmhouse and fields. The fields surrounding the house were inert this season, as they'd been planted specifically for the movie with a strange, high wheat that was essentially decorative and left to grow long past harvesttime. Tonight it blew very dramatically in the cold wind, and under the movie lights it took on some of the same abandon and self-sufficiency and reckless beauty of some movie stars. Apparently James's father had met with some good-natured grief from his neighboring farmers about his willingness to let his fields be taken over for a year by this useless wheat.

I spotted Bram's boxy, stooped frame and went to stand beside him. He nodded at me and returned to watching. The scene they were shooting was simple, just a boy sitting in the glassed-in greenhouse, his head in his hands. This was

131

the boy in the movie who would become the man who would change into a woman whenever feeling overwhelmed him. The crew, about forty people, were all standing nearly breathless as a camera circled the boy. His head still had that delicate, sad weight that young children's heads have, and tilted to the side, it looked as if it might topple him, a Charlie Brown head, a pod atop a slender stalk, full of thoughts, hypotheses, fears.

There was so much silence, and such supernatural light. The fields beyond the greenhouse were waving and waving, and appeared to grow in the light; they seemed to understand this was a performance. The boy looked like he was going to cry. In the script his mother had just died. There was a gladiolus that hung near his head and seemed to incline toward him. I thought of one of the lines from a Michael English fax: "Actually we are intending this to be a movie, not a series of still-lifes." The field bristled—golden, alive. Earlier that day, back in New York as the plane had ascended out of LaGuardia, I had taken quite a few Xanax, adding some more throughout the day, and now they seemed all to kick in at once, compromising the sense of certainty I'd felt when I'd booked this flight. Back in New York, it had seemed so simple: I had money, and James needed money—very hand in glove. But now that I was here, it seemed that money was beside the point. What was needed for a movie was ineffable—something like a common silence among a group of people, as well as a focus so intense that it could slow time, combined with a sort of comatose, disciplined command of the present moment, and also that, well, *tender waiting* that a scene requires. It wasn't until I saw Michael English in the crowd that I came to my senses. I knew it was him right away. He looked amused, detached, slightly annoyed. You could see, even from a distance, his calculating the cost of everything at every moment. Just to see his twitching limbs, I was reminded that of course it actually costs a stupendous amount of money to slow time, to capture even the simplest images. And the klieg light that was bright enough to cleave day from night and that I'd seen from ten miles away? That probably cost close to a thousand dollars every single hour.

Michael English looked great, stylish in a very understated way—plain, beige pants, and a white button-down shirt under a beige, slightly nubby blazer. He was very slender, and there was something orderly and urban about him. He looked traumatized to be in the countryside, his breath in agitated little fogs even inside this greenhouse. He was a person I understood, my type of person, and as James called a wrap, I tried, unsuccessfully, to catch his eye.

30

I found Charley inside, manning huge pots of chili on the stove. She looked of course fantastic and robust. She was clearly trying to downplay her looks and was able to convey both a bohemian actressy look along with a humble young farmer's wife look, a long blond braid down her back coupled with a ginghamy-type dress. She hugged me graciously when she saw me. "Does James know you're here?" she asked.

People were filing in from the shoot. There was music playing already, a party gearing up—everybody coming in from the cold. It reminded me of house parties James and I had attended as undergraduates—warm, beery refuges against the chilly New England winter. Charley called him over and he came toward us in a big unattractive parka and had a knit hat sitting directly on top of his head. He looked quite confused when he saw me but right away he hugged me. "You came! What brings you?"

"I just was curious to see the movie. I decided at the last minute."

"I'm glad. What will the city do without you? You know, I don't think I've ever seen you outside a city—outside Boston or New York."

"I was here," I said. "Before," I added, unwilling to mention his mother's death.

"Oh, oh, yes, of course. I'm sorry." He turned to Charley. "Justine came to my mother's funeral."

She smiled warmly, sympathetically. I didn't feel competitive with Charley, but her lack of jealousy toward me was causing me to feel that my magnanimous attitude regarding her was going to waste. She didn't seem to even notice that James and I had what I had come to call—perhaps overdramatizing—a romantic friendship. I looked around the living room. "It's exactly the same," I said.

"Yeah, it's just how my mother left it. She perfected the look," he said. They had one of those large picture windows that I had always coveted as a child growing up in an apartment. In this case it looked out over the dark and endless expanse of the prairies. In front of it stood the money man Michael English. He looked like somebody's dapper uncle at Thanksgiving. "Is that him?" I asked James. "Is that Michael English, by the way?"

"Yes, I've instructed everybody to ignore him. He's always just standing there by himself."

"It's probably not his fault personally," I said. "He's just doing what the studio tells him."

"No, no. He *is* the studio. I've tried to talk to him; he's like a robot."

"I thought you loved robots," I said. James still mentioned robots frequently in conversation, even now, deep into his adulthood.

"There are all kinds," he said. "Go try to talk to him."

"You give me leave to talk to him?"

James smiled. "I do."

31

~

"It's going to be a beautiful movie," I said. I was next to Michael English, standing before the picture window in which we could see ourselves, dimly, and trace through our translucent bodies the tangled branches of two huge Dutch elms, their arms ghostly and dripping with ice.

"This movie?" he said.

"Yes."

"It'll never get made."

"Yes it will."

"Today we got a shot of a boy's head, one shot of one boy's head."

"I saw that, it was gorgeous."

"Yesterday we got a shot of one person walking across a field."

"I heard about that."

"You know," he said, "life is just not this precious, it's not this valuable. You can't capture every moment. Some moments just rush by, and they, just, there they go."

This made me laugh.

"He wants to cup every moment in his hands," he said.

"Well, he's originally a poet."

"Poets are good. They don't waste anybody's money. The page can await their every thought."

I could see James in the kitchen, scooping off his hat as he bent forward to talk into the back of Charley's thick braid. She was stirring one of the pots on the stove, and she turned when he did this, and reached up to brush the hair from his forehead. Sometimes intimacy looked so strange to me; if you haven't had a relationship in a long time, it seems ridiculous that you can just reach out and touch a person whenever you feel like it.

"Are you staying at the Hotel Saskatchewan?" I asked. I knew he was. Everybody from the movie was staying there, and I was too. It was a big, old-fashioned hotel in the center of Regina.

"Yes."

"When are you going back?"

"I don't know, right away, I guess, as soon as I finish my chili."

"Can I ride with you? There's something I want to discuss."

"Of course, but what?"

"I'll tell you in the cab."

"Okay," he said.

"I happen to believe in this movie," I said. I hadn't intended it to sound so uppity.

"Oh dear," he said.

32

At the center of the city of Regina sits a small, perfectly square park, Victoria Park, surrounded by evergreens. From the lounge of the Hotel Saskatchewan, a person can stare into this park as the first snows fall into it. I told Michael English, as we drank hot, buttery brandy ciders, about the innumerable nights of my girlhood—heartbroken for various teenager reasons—watching the snow fall lazily into Central Park.

"A life of privilege then," he said, but not unkindly.

"My point was that it was beautiful to see the snow fall and here we are seeing it again."

"You're right. I'm sorry. My class envy shows. It's the same snow that falls on all the children."

"Where did you grow up?"

"Westchester."

"Westchester? Oh yes, land of trailer parks."

"There are service people in Westchester. My people have always served. We are butlers at heart."

"Did you notice that you're a studio executive?"

"A very fancy butler, that's all."

"That's ridiculous."

"Look at me standing there every day watching James Nutter ruin his perfectly brilliant script."

"You think the script is brilliant?"

"Yes I do."

"I'm surprised. I thought you were trying to shut it down."

"I've done everything possible to keep him working. I come home to this hotel every night and can't sleep for it."

"James would be surprised. He says he just needs a few more days."

"He needs forever."

"Let me tell you what I have in mind."

By the next morning, after I'd laid out my plan and we'd both slept on it, we had cut a fairly good deal, I thought, and we refined it as we went strolling around downtown Regina, across Victoria Park, past its monument to the world wars, under its enormous blue-green pines, which were so thick and bristling, taking on weight and heft as they prepared to withstand the snowy winter ahead.

Michael English was wearing a longish brown leather jacket and slacks that suggested, just slightly, jodhpurs. He was a supremely good negotiator, able to conceive of deals as win-win, which only the very considerate, their spirits impeccably aligned, can do. I felt very much like we were writing the future as we sat on a little bench and watched pedestrians pass by. Aquinas would support the movie for a brief time and reap nearly double on our investment, and though this was not strictly appropriate according to the tax laws that govern nonprofits, it was in the right spirit, I thought. Later, when other people doubted this, I would as well. But then, it seemed like the only choice. And anyway, not all charity money goes to the downtrodden. And not all should. And how about the woman who poured wine on Jesus' feet while outside the poor begged for food? Wasn't she praised in the end for her devotion, her spiritual recklessness?

33

That night I met James and Charley for dinner at a little
restaurant called the Utopia Café. I arrived first. When
James showed up with Charley they were already deep in an
argument. Charley seemed cool and quite philosophical, but
James was sort of losing his mind over it. He paused to nod
at me as he unwound a scarf from his neck, the one thing
that made me think he must after all be in love with
Charley. His tastes were so simple that even a small black
scarf around his neck looked utterly flamboyant and whim-
sical on him. She had, as always, that confident and super-
human glow that motivational speakers take on, or maybe
that is required to become one. She smiled at me as they sat
down and said one last thing to James. "All I'm saying is that
we do choose, I think we choose our lives." Her hair was
piled on her head in a big, fabulous messy bun with a pencil
stuck through it. She was wearing a sari which mostly you
shouldn't do if you are blond and your people are from
Sweden, but on Charley it looked perfect and natural.

"So, let me put it this way," James continued arguing. "I saw a guy in Bombay once who had to walk around like a crab, that's how messed up his body was. Do you think anybody would choose that?"

"Yes," she said. "I believe we choose the lives we have. Maybe he's learning something in that condition."

"Oh great. So you choose to do your learning in a healthy, well-fed body. Or maybe you don't have any learning to do?"

"I have my difficulties."

"When do they decide?" I asked. "When do people decide?"

"Prior to life," she said. Charley was extremely intelligent but was also the sort of person who, in her need to think positively, said some fairly irrational things. James looked stricken. He basically couldn't tolerate any cosmologies that didn't take into account Bramichari's experience existentially. I'd seen him, even in college classes, attempt to refute any belief systems that couldn't explain Bramichari's limitations, and since it was very difficult to incorporate the unfairness of Bram's life into any system, since his suffering couldn't really be explained, ever, at least on this earth (or anybody's suffering for that matter), the only system that could take him into account was a system that contained inside itself chaos or natural selection, all those cruel systems that leave us without God and with nowhere to go after death, but which included Bramichari equally. James was one of those atheists God must love the most, much more than those of us who were believers, since it is their insistence on fairness and their sensitivity to suffering that make their minds closest to the mercy found in God's mind, but also made them reject any belief in God.

Charley, of course, didn't know any of this. She persisted. "I believe we sign a contract with God. He asks, *will you go?*" Her upper body was wrapped so beautifully in the sari, which fell in lovely horizontal pleats along her chest, and along whose fabric ran a design of swirly-type kidney beans. "God asks," she continued, "and we agree, and so we are put on the earth."

"That's absurd," James said.

"God does ask," she said again. "Everybody gets a choice."

It actually did kind of sound absurd, what she was saying, but then, in my experience, religious ideas only sound good inside one's own brain, whirling around in blood and darkness.

VI

34

~

"By the way, did you give him the money? Did you hand over that money?" Peter asked.

It was a soft, warm morning for November. I was back in New York. I stared at Peter, thinking for a moment that he knew of my trip up to Canada. I considered telling him the truth, and I even felt a bit righteous about it: the Artists' Alliance had spent their money on their self-indulgent dreams, and now it was gone. Now it would support the movies.

"That novelist?" Peter said finally. "Did you give him the money?"

"Oh. No. I wanted to talk to you first."

"That's a switch. Me?"

"You."

"And so?"

"And so?" I repeated.

"And so what did she do?"

"It's very disturbing when you speak of me in the third

person," I said. I found it flattering, though, and thought it meant somehow he might someday want to be in love with me.

"Really," he said.

"As if I'm a problem the two of us are having."

Peter smiled at this.

"Especially when it's so obviously you that's the problem," I went on.

"Me?"

"You." And then a wave of feeling for him overwhelmed me, at that word. "I think Keen wants to use our repaying as evidence against Mr. Burns in court," I said.

"I see."

"So I thought we should give it back only after the trial is over."

"Oh, of course. Okay. Yes, let's."

Yes, let's.

"And now," Peter said. "Do you want to go with me downtown? I told Zhou we'd meet him on the FDR for the fireworks."

"Sure," I said. "Let's go." And the rest of the afternoon flew by as we rode the very crowded subway and then walked from Midtown, where the sun broke through the upper regions of the city's jagged skyline and fell, fractured by human ingenuity, on our heads. This was the proper light by which to see Peter. He loved the city. Sometimes when we lapsed into silence, Peter sang under his breath one of his little songs of language. There was a Russian ditty he sang, an old prayer for children that he translated for me one day into "I fold my little hands so small." It seemed sweet and a little too tragically about the passing of time to hear Peter sing it, his own hands so spidery and long, his fingers folding over awkwardly whenever he clasped them together.

"Remember last year?" Peter said to Zhou after we caught up with him on the FDR, standing under a preordained lamppost. It was right before the fireworks began. "Remember that?" Peter went on. "When we were here and you blew those bubbles out of your nose?"

"That was funny," I said. The three of us had been in this exact spot last year for the fireworks. Zhou had swallowed a Coke incorrectly, and bubbles had come out of his nose.

"No," Zhou said. "No bubbles."

"Zhou," Peter said. "I saw it happen with my own eyes."

"No," Zhou said.

"Look, this isn't China. You can't just say things didn't happen so that they will unhappen," Peter said.

"Peter!" I said. China rose before us all, I think, with its beauty, its sublime mind control.

"It didn't happen in the first place," Zhou said.

"It happened," Peter said under his breath, so as to get in the last word before the fireworks began—a single spark launched from the other side of the river that tore quietly,

148

invisibly through the sky and exploded over us. I watched for a while and then turned to see Zhou's reaction, and he was crying, his face tilted toward the sky. It was impossible for me to know how he felt. Zhou was a very explicit type of casualty under Mao—a Red Guard, a *child* Red Guard. He had been raised into the Red Guard as a schoolchild, and he had been turned, as many children of landlords were, against his own father. (Peter had told me this and had extracted from me a promise never to discuss it with Zhou, as it was the chief unhappiness of his life.) Zhou had been forced to attend criticisms against his own father, and he had even, on one occasion, joined the Red Guards as they raided the family home, looking for evidence of capitalist tendencies.

Or maybe it had nothing to do with his father. It was probably about Yiang-Yang. It's an old story: she was back in the basin of the Yangtze, and he was in New York City. They were in love, but both of them were so stoic about their situation that I never thought of it as a hardship for them. The Chinese excel at long-distance relationships, after all, and calculate miles with more patience than the rest of the world. The Chinese in love will tolerate any distance at all, said the work of the great Italo-fascist Sinophile Ezra Pound. The Ming and the Yuan dynasties in particular believed that love can be proved only by distance, and this belief lasted literally down through the ages, and then, in the time of Zhou and Yiang-Yang, it became coupled with a particularly Communist notion of the state over the individual, all of which made of China's young Communist lovers great warriors of time and space, their family lives strung across great distances, the inner eye full of long reaches of landscape. When one's lover is far away, apparently the mind becomes enormous, and has within it at all times a magnificent journey.

35

On certain mornings, if the mist was mixing auspiciously with the milky light of the rising sun, the city was invisible for a brief time, the tops of the Twin Towers exactly the color of the breaking day. I was in the office early, working on the books. My biggest problem, in the wake of my giving over three hundred thousand dollars to the movie, was not in keeping Aquinas afloat; that's fairly easy to do, run an organization for a time on thin air alone. People do this all the time, toss operations airborne, where they float, briefly, without money, like in the cartoons when somebody runs off a cliff and hovers atmospherically before he falls. My real problem was that I had a board meeting coming up in two weeks, when I would basically have to lay bare the books. Most of the members were not that particular, but two of them were extremely vigilant, and almost impossible to put one over on. One of them happened to be Tom Selleck, of *Magnum, P.I.* fame, and the other was a vice president of GE by the name of Amy Celica. Almost every meeting was another facedown with Amy, who had pioneered ready-to-spread frosting, and Tom Selleck. So this morning I was trying to figure out a way either to hide the transaction from them or to convince them it was a "reasonable investment," which is how the law breaks along what a charity can do with donor money. Of course, our main donor, Mr. Burns, would have been delighted if the money was going to the movies, but what Mr. Burns or any donor wanted us to do with the money was far outstripped by what the IRS required us to do with it in order to remain in their eyes a charity.

I still felt as certain about the movie, and lending Aquinas's support to it, as I had standing under that powerful, trembling light up on the prairies, but that didn't make it any easier to convince the numbers to agree back in the city. Numbers are the epitome of honesty and resist manipulation. I easily had two hundred and twenty thousand dollars, but the last hundred or so thousand was very hard to come by. And I had to disguise all the activity in the books. I was still struggling at nine-thirty A.M. when Peter entered the office.

"Ni-hao," he said.

I lifted my head, and the city leapt out of its milky dawn, into shape and permanence. "Hi, Peter."

He settled immediately into his morning habit—sitting down at his desk and preparing his little blood-counting machine to measure the constituents of his blood—its density, its tide and spray.

"You're so studious this morning," he said. "What are you doing?"

"Just numbers, nothing exciting."

"How's your young man?"

"He's fine. He's not really mine, actually. He's gone—directing a movie up in Canada."

"I'll have to meet him." He pricked his finger, placed it above the glucose counter, and then in the thirty or so seconds it took for the machine to determine the sugar in his blood, he stood beside me, leaning over my desk, looking out the window into the city. I tried casually to close up the books, not that he would discern at a glance what was under way within.

"If you two are serious," he continued.

"No, you need to quit saying that. We're just friends, basically. Sorry."

Peter shrugged, then addressed his blood on the beeping glucose counter. I turned back to the books. What they would show was that, for these three or four months, operations at Aquinas were proceeding as usual, but then in a shadow book I kept, a leathery old dream diary, the true situation was revealed, which was that I'd taken nearly all the money I'd siphoned off to give back to the miserable, self-righteous Artists' Alliance, as well as money from several other of Aquinas's accounts, and used it to write a check to the movie in the amount of three hundred thousand dollars. The books would reveal that the person in charge of the books was a bit of an artist herself! Moving the world around, shaping it, not just supporting it. Of course, an equally reasonable interpretation might be that she was risking money that was not hers to risk and attempting to run an organization without any money really, assuming that what was given would come back, the assumption based on the ephemeral hopes and dreams that accompany movies and maybe also any work of art.

At the end of the day, I went out to get some Chinese soup for Peter and me. When I returned, I found Peter on the phone. I put on my own headset and stood beside him. It was the Gripper from L.A., now insisting that his client's name be in the actual title of the Noodle House, his client's ridiculous, somewhat household, movie-star name.

I looked over at Peter to roll my eyes and saw he was now shielding his eyes from the dying light. Occasionally Peter's sight started to go late in the day. Some scar tissue had formed years ago on his retinas, because of his diabetes, and when this scar tissue had healed, it shrank, pulling the retinal layers apart, so that when he became tired, images would break loose from their moorings and flap a little in the breeze.

"It's not possible," I broke into the conversation.

"Oh, it's you," the Gripper said.

"It obviously doesn't look good for a star to have his name on anything resembling a hospital," I said. "It makes him look like a megalomaniac. I'm surprised you'd even consider this."

"Look," he said, "at this point anything would look better than for my client to be mixed up with a rinky-dink little organization like this." And he hung up.

I looked over at Peter, who was somewhat hunched over his desk. I led him to the couch and laid him down. I turned off all the lights and sat beside him as the day mercifully darkened. He was lying on his side, with his back to the wall, and I was sitting inside the crook of his body. He had his eyes closed. I often sat with him when this happened, in case he suddenly needed a shot or something. I loved these minutes. I suppose it's true that these were his most vulnerable moments, when his body was mostly overrunning its limits, and for me to be reading romance into this stillness wasn't exactly healthy or even that kind, really. Still, it gave me peace, and I always felt that maybe he had feelings for me as well, and this quiet time was their expression. Our soup went cold. The sun went down. I felt the day's anxiety dissipating.

After ten or so minutes, he said, "You want to eat some pizza with me?"

"Sure," I said. "That would be good."

"On Thompson?"

"Yeah, great." And then, as soon as we stood up, the phone rang one last time. I picked up the regular phone instead of the headset.

"Justine?" It was David League. "This is a courtesy call."

"Yes?"

"I'm putting you on notice, I will report Aquinas's practices to the *New York Times* within fourteen days if you do not pay back that money."

"This is none of your business."

"I will do this. You have two weeks. I trust you'll come up with a solution in that time. I can't stand back and let these victims suffer anymore."

"These victims," I said. "You mean you. You the victim."

I saw Peter looking at me with some curiosity. "I'll call you back," I said.

"Fine."

"Who was that?" Peter asked immediately. "Call who back?"

"It's nothing. Let's go eat."

"Tell me."

The very last, dim light of day was still hanging in our office, as Peter and I sat there amid the dark forms of my file cabinets and his spindly easels, our big orange couch just holding us there, quietly suspended hundreds of feet above the earth. *Teach us to sit still, even among these rocks.*

"Come on," I said. "Let's go."

On the corner of Thompson and Spring, we ate our slices at a little cement table outside. Peter's eyesight was gradually returning to normal, and now he kept tapping my knee with his own and leaning toward me, asking me what was going on. He didn't seem alarmed or upset, really, just curious. And his curiosity looked not unlike attraction, I noticed. Maybe this was what happened when you embezzled money from a man. Maybe it was one of those aphrodisiacs that you stumble on sometimes, left over from the times when only men could own property, so that just as a man will pour his earthly resources into a woman he loves, so it might also work in the reverse; that is, if you can figure out a way to get his resources on your own, his poor, overdetermined heart will have no choice but to follow.

36

I've always felt that if there's no God, it all could just go down the drain for all I care. I know this is not a noble belief, and makes me a sort of Christian nihilist, if there is such a category, and I know the world itself, apart from its maker, is so interesting that even if it is all by accident, it's worth praising. For me, though, if you take a god out from behind the scenes, it's all just empty puppets, silly and slack, dreaming of heaven. Therefore my most fervent prayers have always been only that God exists, and also heaven.

"It's a bit circular, your reasoning, isn't it?" Cinnamon said to me after I'd expressed this. Cinnamon was one of Bonnie-Beth's best friends from their Barnard days, and we were all three having coffee. Cinnamon was very cool and practical. She was currently a professor of political theory at a small religious college in Minnesota and was driven a little crazy by it—both the Midwest itself and all the Lutherans in whose midst she lived and breathed. "It would be interesting if it turns out there is a God, but it doesn't seem likely," Cinnamon said.

Bonnie-Beth pulled back dramatically from the table at this and looked upward while pointing at Cinnamon. Bonnie-Beth was quite superstitious and had a very complicated relationship with a sort of Old Testament God who was always trying to outsmart her and keep her from heaven. "She said it, I didn't say it," Bonnie-Beth said.

Cinnamon was in town to continue an affair she'd begun with a married Fordham professor she'd met at a conference, and we had spent the last hour strategizing with her regarding how to get him to leave his wife. In order to allow ourselves to do this we had worked ourselves into a lather over how terrible his wife was—too acquisitive, too artificial, too superficial—though none of us knew her except through the words of her husband, as repeated by Cinnamon. Our conversations were a triumph of friendship over morality. We were at Dean & DeLuca on Prince Street, right around the corner from my apartment, in a big warehouse that passes for nice in the Village. There were currently two celebrities in the café—Robert Sean Leonard and Matthew Broderick. They were in separate groups, but each came in accompanied by the little frisson of energy that surrounds celebrity, just like my little pizza shop on the corner of Thompson and Spring, which took on a whole new aura after it had appeared in a movie, after it had distinguished itself as something worth putting down on film for all time, even though the movie itself, everyone agreed, was awful.

At any rate, I wished I could be as analytical and honest as Cinnamon regarding belief in God, but I had a wheel that spun inside, set there by my parents, and everything good was attached to it, like streamers in the wind.

I had laid on the table some Xeroxes of Peter's sketches for the Noodle House, since Cinnamon had asked to see them. I was quite proud of them, and of the project in general, when it came down to it, even though I considered the possibility of it ever existing remote at best. Peter's drawings were beautiful and personal and genuine. They had that paradoxical combination of fragile and indestructible that Christopher Alexander said was at the heart of any good building, any good *anything*, actually, according to him.

I noticed the light was falling in nearly horizontally— neon orange—breaking into the café, signaling that I was late to meet Peter, so I left immediately, kissing them both, wishing Cinnamon luck on her date later that evening with the hopefully soon-to-be-separated professor, and headed out into the crush of a Friday-night crowd on Broadway. Twenty minutes later, I was turning on foot from Hudson to Canal, where everything was blackened by the last of the red and falling sun, including Peter's approaching figure, which I watched come toward me, into shape, then form, then being. He was wearing a tux, which made him look taller than usual. He smiled, kissed my hand. "Beloved," he said, which had begun long ago as a Mr. Burns imitation but had stayed on as a legitimate way to greet each other. And then we walked together across Canal, and then down Mott, and on toward Water Street and the party, which was to take place halfway between Chinatown and the sea.

When we arrived, there was nobody greeting us at the door. The invitation had said this was a dinner party for leaders in nonprofit, and though it was sponsored by *Fortune* magazine, no actual person seemed to be emerging as host. We just knocked; somebody leaned back from the table and let us in.

Since we were, as usual, late, the guests were already seated around a huge table in the apartment, which was on the fortieth floor. Beyond the table were banks of windows, revealing every type of water imaginable in the dusky light—bays and inlets, rivers, the ocean, even the glittering, hepatitis-ridden Gowanus in the distance. The windows were open, so that there was an evening mist even inside. This, as well as the huge scarred-wood table that dominated the room, and the chandelier just slightly swaying above, was suggestive of the fact that Manhattan is an island and, as such, heir to the vulnerabilities of islands—dependence on water, subtle movement, eventual vanishing.

Peter and I sat in two chairs on the northeast side of the table. We recognized a few people, who waved or shouted mild merriments. Christopher Robin was there; he nodded our way even as he continued to charm everybody within a six-foot radius. *Smile and smile,* I thought, *still the villain.* There was a happy, buoyant feeling at the table, which was covered already with appetizers, plates of food all cultivated into roses—ham roses, carrot roses, squash roses, roast beef roses, cucumber roses.

"So," Peter said to the woman across from us. "There's a fancy mind behind the meal."

She smiled at him luminously, lifted her goblet. I recognized her then as Allison Glass, who'd become somewhat famous in nonprofit circles for turning around the financial fate of the Girl Scouts. I'd met her once before, and now I introduced her to Peter. I hadn't realized before how pretty she was, pretty in a sort of irritating way. She looked like the soul of organization, as if the categories inside of her had all been filled, as if that's what beauty was, that kind of fulfillment.

"And so you are the famous Allison Glass," Peter said. "Creating money out of thin air they say."

At that moment, as the first stirrings of jealousy arose in me, somebody put a hand on my shoulder. It was the woman to my right, a very statuesque woman with a big, complicated shelf of a chest, all systematized by a series of pulleys and wires. She was instantly warm and generous, some extraordinary god's idea of a woman—*Blood of His Blood,* as Emily Dickinson would say. When she said her name in introduction—Lady Highgrave, so clearly a nom de plume, so clearly the name of somebody who had drastically changed her life, suggesting as it did both death and joy—it occurred to me, in a rush of certainty, that Lady Highgrave was, or had been at one time, a man.

"He is your husband," she said to me, nodding at Peter, as we both watched him talk to Allison Glass.

"Oh, we aren't married," I said.

"You are engaged to him?"

"Just friends."

"Ah, a friend." She looked at me smartly, secretly. "So you are not married to anyone?"

"No," I said. "And you?"

"No, but I wish I were," she said, buoyantly.

"I'm sure you will someday," I said.

"Yes," she said. Of all of her, only her neck and jaw looked like a man's. "Someday he'll lift his head and there I'll be, his unexpected bride."

And then I noticed, lifting his old weather-beaten head, Francis Efferveti, halfway down the table. I was surprised: I hadn't noticed him when we first sat down. God, in this light his skin looked completely ruined. He looked like an old Scandinavian—Grieg or Ibsen, some old person whose skin had evolved for northern weather and instead had been made to endure the sun of Africa and Southeast Asia. He had that lonely look that some international people take on—worldly and lonely—exquisitely, elegantly lonely. I'd always thought of him as so vital and spry, with a missionary's zeal—thin, ascetic, nearly dispersing before your eyes, more of a *quality* really than a person who lived in the world, a quality of, in Francis's case, goodness at any cost, of the world to come over and against this world.

"Justine," he mouthed, and pursed his lips in a kiss. I felt a tightness in my chest at the thought of him and Peter being in the same room, not only because they hated each other but because I had never told Peter that it was Francis who had helped us move the Noodle House. So, with rising anxiety, I turned back to the other problem at hand: Peter's having an intimate conversation with Allison. Even their names fit together perfectly—Peter and Allison. I couldn't bear the thought that she was what Peter might want in a woman—there were no trials burning up in her, just a long series of problems solved.

"When I came aboard," Allison was saying to Peter, "almost all our financial base was predicated on cookie sales." Peter was listening intently. I saw him reach then for a cucumber rose and begin to tear off one layer with his teeth. His hand was shaking slightly, which worried me a little, both for his blood sugar's sake and because I could see Allison at that moment clueing in on it, becoming attracted to it. *It's rude of you to find it attractive,* I wanted to say to her. *It's an infirmity.*

"When the false rumors came out in the mid-eighties," Allison continued, "about razor blades in the cookies, it shattered the organization's finances. By the time I arrived, they were still laboring under the idea that the girls should be involved in every aspect of raising money. I got the girls out of there and began to actually invest."

"Maybe the girls could have learned to invest," I said. "Maybe gotten a badge for it."

"No," Allison said, flatly. "They're too young to invest."

"Oh, of course," said Peter.

"Those cookies," she went on. "Can you imagine what kind of shaky financial empire was built of those cookies? I'd just as soon do without them altogether. Does anybody eat them?"

"Everybody eats them," I said.

"I love the Thin Mints," Peter said.

"The mints are the best sellers," she said, nodding and taking a sip of her wine. "I wouldn't mind just selling the Thin Mints, repackaging them into smaller packages, and maybe go into mail order, so we don't have to bother with the girls going door-to-door, which is becoming difficult, not to mention dangerous."

"Maybe just do away with the girls altogether," I said.

She smiled at me. We hated each other. Fortunately, Peter was suddenly preoccupied with something down the long table. He had spotted Efferveti.

"And how is everything at Aquinas?" Allison asked us.

"It's fine," I said.

"Yes, it's great," Peter said, tearing his eyes away from Ef-ferveti.

"Was your budget affected by the new nonprofit rulings?"

"That's Justine's area," Peter said. "The budget."

"Our budget?" I said. "It's a house of cards."

We all laughed mildly, as if it were a joke. But then Allison looked at me profoundly, knowingly, with her greeny, mermaid eyes. "I've been there," she said, very sincerely. And I fell for her a little myself, had a moment of fellow feeling. It would be comforting to believe that somebody like her had once collapsed a budget with a series of bad decisions, pulling down with her everybody she loved, and then somehow had eventually arisen out of such chaos and failure to sit before us with a beauty made up almost entirely of order.

"How is Justine then?" Francis cried out, with a kind of decadent ease.

"I'm fine," I said. "You?"

"Excellent. And Peter." He nodded at Peter. "Don't tell me you two are a couple now?"

I thought this might be a good moment to stick it to Allison Glass, by not denying this, so I just smiled and looked at my plate, but Peter quickly refuted it. "Justine and I are working together on a project in China."

"That's right," Francis said. "Your new project. It sounds perfectly charming and useless to the Chinese people."

"It isn't useful in the way, say, you were useful in China," said Peter.

"Do you mean *useful* as it is commonly used, for example, giving years of one's life to helping an entire nation know God?"

"Yes, that's exactly the sort of uselessness I'm speaking of."

This argument was so tired, and it got played out every time you had a missionary and an aid worker in the same room—do you give people bread or do you give them the Gospel? But fortunately, Peter and Francis silenced themselves at this point, before it got too absurd. The last thing Peter wanted, I knew, was for them to be shouting theology across the table like two crazies. So, after a tense moment, dinner proceeded. It seemed that Efferveti was willing to not tell Peter that he'd been instrumental in moving the Noodle House, but still I was nervous. I didn't quite trust him in this regard; he wasn't exactly the type to hide his light under a bushel. I could still picture him walking up our little lane in our old Beijing neighborhood, that very fertile, orange-blossomy, and as it turned out terrifying landscape, which now seemed to me like someplace I'd known in a children's book, though a book that I'd loved so deeply that it was more my life than my life had ever been. The periphery of Beijing, where we lived, was so beautiful—high sycamores, which Confucius called the tree of heaven and which Mao renamed the tree of life, and the steady, peaceful Yangtze moving endlessly out to sea. Yet if you could crack open Beijing in the early seventies, you would see the damage that people of enormous goodwill can do. Initially, Mao was the hero-scholar of all China. He saved China from the brutal reign of the emperors. Even in the West, Mao was championed. China had stepped into the modern world, led by the striding, self-reliant Mao. But by increments, Mao himself changed, became paranoid, and fragile in that way the powerful are; he couldn't be told that any of his far-flung schemes—the Great Leap Forward, a Hundred Flowers Blooming, the Proletariat Revolution—were failing. And he became as brutal as, and more so than, the emperors and the Kuomintang he had unseated. Even after all these years of historical scholarship, however, it's impossible to say exactly when the good began to turn bad. 1970? 1971? When did the badness creep in? Or, more accurately, when did whatever goodness Mao promulgated no longer justify the amount of badness?

Peter could not get me out of that party fast enough, for which I for one was happy. I had one more aperitif, some more roses stolen quickly, one slow, unexpected dance with a man named Bryce, and then Peter and I were gone. "Life is short," he said as we stepped into the elevator and floated down the forty stories to sea level again.

37

Peter and I walked home, up the inside of the island, and landed in my apartment on Thompson. I put on hot water to make tea and clicked on my messages. First my mother, who happened to include a hello to Peter, which she often did—"Hello to Peter!" Peter smiled, waved at the machine. And then there was a message from James: "Justine, everything is ramping up here again. The studio is letting us shoot our last scenes. Bram and I were to leave for New York tomorrow, but now I have to stay. Bram wants to fly anyway, without me. Will you pick him up at LaGuardia and escort him to Lester Hotel? I'll be back a day or so later, probably on Saturday. Thanks! Call me."

"That's your young man?" Peter asked, settling his long, grasshoppery limbs into my low armchair. I passed him his tea and sat down across from him. Sometimes I would do something like this, pass him green tea, and in my gesture unfurling I felt Su Chen, some memory of her pass through my body.

"He's not so young," I said.

"Who is Bram?"

"His brother."

"Sounds like it's serious between you two."

"It's not, and anyway, since we're asking who's who, why are you so dead set against me speaking to Francis?"

"Francis is everybody's worst enemy."

"Meaning?"

"Meaning stay away from him, please. He's the sort of person whose goodwill will kill you. Now that he's seen you, he'll be calling. But you must say no if he wants to meet with you."

"Sure," I said. I didn't want to set Peter's blood sugar running again. But of course I knew Francis much better than Peter knew I did. I'd had dinner with him many times at my parents' apartment without telling Peter. I'd had many conversations with him, and I knew all about him trying to remove Su Chen from China. I knew all about it! When I was a child, I saw events in China happen as through a veil, but I saw clearly now.

38

Before meeting with Bramichari, I met again with David League in a restaurant on Jones Street. He had requested this visit earlier in the week. I found him there when I arrived, in a plush maroon chair at a table by the window. His hair was feathered beautifully, and that combined with his trim beard suggested Kris Kristofferson, or maybe one of the Bee Gees. I was lulled briefly into the feeling that we were on a date.

He gestured toward the bottle of wine as I sat down and raised his eyebrows.

"Thank you," I said. "Yes."

"So," he said as he poured, "you said when you called that indeed you would be returning some of the money to the victims." I found the word *victims* a bit irritating in this context but ignored it.

"Yes, soon."

"How soon?"

"Six months." This would be long after the trial was over,

and Keen would then not be able to use our returning it as a plank in his offense against Mr. Burns. And anyway, at present the money was tied up. It had another adventure first, in the form of a major Hollywood production, and after that, after it had doubled itself, it could go back to the artists.

David League looked at me mournfully. "So you've arrogated this position for yourself—deciding when it is the victims should get their money back."

"No," I said. "I'm simply trying to correct the situation without destroying our charity. Right now, removing it would do irredeemable damage."

"This money is bloody. Certainly it's not performing any good deeds at this moment."

"Actually it is. And all money is bloody. The virtue lies in how it is spent."

"That's a terrifying little motto, perfect for money-laundering operations. What I meant was bloody was your charity."

Our waiter approached and took our appetizer orders. This was going to be a long meal.

"Anyway," League continued, "it's not your decision as to when they should get the money back. It's their money. It's theirs."

I had spent a few days poring over the financial records of these artists for Mr. Burns, so I knew a little something of their personalities. These people were not victims; they had laid out money their whole lives in service of their dreams, and as anybody knows, this is a costly way to live, with fewer financial returns. But the joys and freedoms of that life are incalculable, and there is a kind of deep pleasure in giving all one has, is, for potentially nothing. And this willingness to risk lent their lives a certain romance, but it was a romance predicated on the fact that if you were this kind of person you had to lose a lot, since losing is central to the experience, and that very loss brings with it wisdom, freedom, perspicacity, and a new tolerance for loss, which in turn makes possible deeper risks and deeper pleasures, all of which is obviously worth any amount of money. I had come to know this personality intimately, and loved it above all others, in the form of Peter. And I knew that it canceled out the benefits of their particular personalities if they then ran to the courts in a fit of litigiousness and a sudden reverence for fairness, of all things.

"It's their money," he continued. "They need it. I am in contact with these people. They have nothing. One of them can't even buy shoes for his child. It's their money. It's not up to you to decide."

"It *was* their money," I said, sounding crazy, even to myself. "The best thing for these people would be to take their desperate little legal action and throw it into the sea. Maybe then their art will take on some significance."

"Why're you so bitter? Are you a bitter person?"

Suddenly the restaurant looked horribly and overly romantic, all decked out in red velvet. And as in romance, I felt as if the only reasonable response to this sort of exasperation was to flee; yet there were strings attached to our relationship, the most significant being his threat to expose Aquinas to the *Times*.

This was the sort of restaurant that served so-called comfort foods: meat loaf and mashed potatoes, but with some insane Manhattan addition—plum confit, cinnamon bark inside the potatoes, and the truly awful basil in the cheesecake. It was the early nineties, when chefs took it upon themselves to mix very promiscuously dessert with dinner and stud all foods with their opposites. The whole meal, in all its contents, was very disconcerting, but I stayed through every permutation of it, promising David League at every turn that in due time he would get his money, which he could then redistribute to the Artists' Alliance—the weavers and sculptors, the potters, the poets, the painters, the, in one instance, jugglers—so they could continue with their conversations, as I'd heard one writer describe it, with the divine, their little negotiations with the universe, their crybaby games.

39

My issue with League unresolved, I finally fled the restaurant to go get Bram at the airport. One hour later, I was at Gate 75, out of which stepped wonderful, unchanging Bramichari, Manhattan rising behind his blocky head. "Bram," I said. "I'm so glad to see you." I hugged him, which he seemed to endure. Bram didn't have any of the excitement a regular person would have, or pretend to have, at greeting somebody. I found this comforting actually.

Generally Bram stayed on the Upper East Side at Lester's, which was a large bed-and-breakfast for travelers who for various psychological reasons couldn't quite be left on their own. Since the curfew was past for Lester's, we had agreed that he would stay one night in my apartment.

Eventually we reached Thompson Street, and after a long, mostly silent walk around my neighborhood, we ascended the many steps to my apartment. I noticed that whenever Bram passed over thresholds he did so with some hesitation; he paid his respects to their uncertainty each time. We listened to my answering machine. There was a hello from James and then, strangely, a message from Francis, telling me that I was invited to a party the next evening at his home. "Have you heard?" he said. "Nixon's dead. He died today. So we're having a fancy dress party. Will you come?"

I turned on my television immediately. One of the networks was playing old newsreels of Nixon, and Bram and I spent the evening watching the grainy, nostalgic images pass across the screen. It was like an interesting book all of us had once read together—Watergate, California in the 1970s, Pat waving, miniskirts, blazer knit sets, lemon trees, Kent State in chaos, Nixon weeping, walking up and down the stairs to his jet planes, waving farewell, Nixon with Kissinger, with Chuck Colson, with the Beatles, with Zhou Enlai, and Mao, with Pol Pot, Nixon at the podium in Asbury Park, high, shaking trees behind him, their leaves rising in steppes into the night sky, and then racing along behind Nixon a streaker, the streaker's long, strange, sinewy body crossing the stage so beautifully, the body giving itself over to the times: the very image—high-stepping, slender, long, feathered hair, limbs *free*—of 1973.

40

Seven hours later, the alarm woke us. We ate muffins from a nearby bakery and drank hot chocolate. The air was cool as we walked to the subway together and waited at its southern entrance for Bonnie-Beth. By ten A.M., after a subway and a cab ride, we were all three knocking on the door of Lester's, which was in a brownstone on East Eighty-eighth, one of those streets that look exactly like the streets of New York in children's books—narrow, intimate streets with trees like patches of watercolor all about.

Once the proprietress checked us in, she showed us around the hotel. After that Bram took me immediately to the ornate, wood-paneled library, with rows of tables lined up the middle, whose feet where they met the floor were the paws of beasts. There were ceiling-high stacks of books. The library was full of people, though completely quiet. Many of the guests at Lester's appeared to be high-functioning autistics—people with what is now referred to as Asperger's—a group most of whom tend to be highly intelligent, bookish, very private, socially disinclined, fanatics to complicated systems of all sorts, devoted to routine, and usually only occasionally employing some of the more outward, flamboyant mannerisms of autistics—the flapping hands, the tiny leaps in the air. This would not have been Bram's diagnosis, exactly, but he seemed to me to be on the same spectrum—highly intelligent and emotionally eccentric.

Eventually it became clear that Bram had no interest in leaving the library, so Bonnie-Beth and I left for lunch, promising to return later in the day.

We ate at the Boathouse and then took a walk around the little pond with the little sailboats. Bonnie-Beth, fresh off another Dr. Michael session, told me about his newest mental exercise, which required one to establish a place Dr. Michael called "the room before the pain," the last place a person had been before the great pain in their life occurred. One could then return there in memory, consciously, again and again, and make of one's mind a peaceful place.

"But there are so many painful things in life, who can think of their one great pain?" I asked.

"You can. Everybody can. Just ask yourself; you can do it."

It was true. Like magic Su Chen appeared in my mind, alive, back in our little galley kitchen, folding in the tiny wings of game hens, humming her little propaganda songs.

"And yours?" I asked. "Do you know yours?" We were walking at the edge of the pond and I realized that we were

in the middle of a crowd of children—New York City children, to be specific, whose cries of alarm and joy were ring-
ing through the park. I winced at my own question.
Bonnie-Beth had miscarried very far into her pregnancy,
late enough for the baby to already make inroads into all of
our lives, Bonnie-Beth's to a degree I would never be able to
measure. I myself had imagined taking the child to all the
places I had once loved—the carousel, the adventure playground, the Bethesda Fountain, the cupcake factory, the
natural history museum—and more than that I'd fancied
myself a sort of aunt, or a governess to the girl, an amah, her
Su Chen, somebody both more indulgent and more sternly
insistent on her self-esteem than a mother, somebody to
teach her to have faith in herself, to ignore the world's judgment, to take up arms against whatever—to use Whitman's
phrase—insults your soul, and to through it all be generous
inside and out. This was *jiangling,* of course.

41

~

Someday he'll lift his head and there I'll be, his unexpected bride. This was exactly what was running through my mind the next evening when I ran into Peter at sunset, on the street outside our building. He'd been gone that day, at a teaching seminar. I was on my way to Francis's, wearing a black evening dress that I kept at work for emergency fundraisers or parties, or, as it turned out in this case, wakes. It was made of tiny metallic scales sewn together, whose effect was supposed to be mermaidy, though this was difficult to carry off. "Oh," he said. "Where are you going, like this?"

"On a date, actually," I lied.

"Good for you," he said, which I found irritating.

The whole time I'd worked for Peter we'd never once met here, outside, where the river curved in, then quickly out again on its way to sea. This corner off the street was always permeated with the smell of the river, which was really the smell of fish in various stages of living and dying and decay and subsequent resurrection. It smelled like time's effect on a river, or really, just like time itself. Say you wanted at last to smell time, you might smell the Hudson River of New York City, standing where Peter and I stood.

"With whom?" he asked.

"Oh, just this guy I know."

"The Canadian?"

"Well, yes."

"Where are you going?"

"To a show."

"Which show?"

"I don't know."

"He didn't tell you?"

"He's like that."

"You look lovely," Peter said, which made me sad. Peter's manners were such that they protected other people from his true feelings, which were often sad and I think lonely. Bonnie-Beth didn't really have any patience for this explanation. She was stouthearted, completely convinced of every person's ability to overcome things, so her sympathy was inflected with a real can-do attitude on their behalf. If a ton of bricks fell on somebody's head, Bonnie-Beth would be willing to feel bad for them, but short of that, she believed in a person's duty to surmount anything, which could make her at times your very best advocate in the face of difficulty and at other times a brutal friend, with an emotionally exacting and practical eye. And my waiting for Peter, and my explaining in very complicated, intricate ways his inability to love me finally just bored her. She couldn't see that all of the pain inside him was still liquid, and filled him to the brim, and even just a little over, and his solitude, his romantic aloofness toward me was a kind of gentleness, a way to not let the liquid spill over, into me, into Aquinas, into our quiet, chaste life together.

42

"Any gathering of two or more," Aquinas wrote, "ought to be fraught with the love of life." It should raise up human life, make it acceptable and interesting to God. And this principle seemed doubly important tonight, since this was a wake, one of many throughout the city tonight to raise the soul of Richard Nixon. And truly, when I walked into Francis's apartment, on the thirty-fourth floor, a mood of total celebration drifted over me. Some people were wearing Nixon masks, and they drifted through the crowd eerily. Long before he was president, or even fully an adult, Nixon had loved China. He had dreamt of China for a good thirty years before he went there finally in 1972, to meet with a by-then very sick and bloated Mao. Nixon was a Sinophile; he was one of those people who spring up in every country—in Canada, in Sweden, in England—people for whom the deepest journey is always, from the beginning, to China, whether they actually ever go there or not.

Francis's apartment was stark and lacquered, black and

white, with long lotus-y plants arching everywhere, sort of a phony, designer rendition of a Chinese aesthetic. I couldn't spot him at first, but then at once, Francis, part missionary, part politico, who'd had, in his lifetime, Nixon's ear, and probably Mao's, and certainly Deng's, was whispering in mine. "You've come then," he said.

"Hi," I said.

"It's surprising to me each time I see you, that you've grown up. Into a woman."

"I guess."

"And under Peter's thumb."

"Well." I smiled. "It only seems that way occasionally."

"Yes, well, he's a charming man."

"Like yourself," I said. I meant this to be a sort of witty compliment, but maybe I also meant to suggest his placement in the same boat as Peter. What boat that was I wasn't quite sure—the boat of charity as self-aggrandizement maybe, the boat of a disturbing charm, of an aloof sort of worldly loneliness.

"How do your parents feel, that their old friend Peter is now in love with you?"

My eyes nearly filled with tears at this. It was silly. When Peter had left China, his boat had trouble turning around in our alcove of the great South China Sea, so it sputtered about in the tiny harbor, churning up water. It looked like a huge and troubled beast caught in a small pond. Peter stood on the deck and waved good-bye for at least twenty minutes. He just kept waving and waving, and I did too. In retrospect, Su Chen had just disappeared, and it's a miracle that Peter was even standing, let alone waving and calling farewell. I would have waved forever. At one point I threw up over the railing, and my parents tried to pull me away and take me home, but I grabbed on to the railing and held on. And then I managed to stand up again and regain my composure and dignity so that Peter would think of me not as a baby but as somebody of whom he could be proud, and to whom he might one day return.

And then tonight, to my right, there was the smell of rain and a hand at my elbow. *Peter.* There were tiny, dewy raindrops on his leather jacket. He'd followed me.

"What are you doing here?" he said to me.

"It's a party," I said.

"What are you doing?" Peter turned to Francis.

"Justine and I are catching up, as old friends do," Francis said, looking at me smartly, and smiling, as if I were very young. "She's explaining your project on the Yangtze. I'm just wondering, who will benefit? It sounds like a playground for the wealthy."

"It will be a playground for the most skilled people in the combination of Western and Eastern medicine."

"And who will benefit?"

"They will, as well as their clients."

"Who no doubt are very wealthy."

"Some are," Peter said. I was surprised that he was engaging in any of this sort of talk, which normally he referred to as "brochure-speak."

"Yes, well, that's your specialty, isn't it? Helping those who don't need it. It's a bit of an illusion for you, isn't it? I mean, for you. It's obviously some sort of edifice to your failure in China."

"If I build out of any responsibility, to the dead or to the living, what concern is that of yours?"

"You were not the only one who loved Su Chen."

This statement was a physical assault on Peter; he was shaking by now. These thoughts had the power to nearly destroy a man of Peter's constitution, pouring into his bloodstream adenosine and adrenaline, both of which require enormous amounts of insulin to manage, in Peter's case all of his very short supply, and this left his blood sugar free to tear through the body—at first like a kind of largesse of the spirit, a willingness to put forward the self with a near total confidence and fundamentalism, but eventually topping out in a kind of hysteria, then fragility, which the body registers by a slight tremor in the hands.

"Do you think we can't see right through your self-righteousness to the corruption at the heart of you?" Peter asked, sounding insane. "You stand naked before us."

This was for sure the blood sugar talking. It sounded

ridiculous, and it was the sort of thing it was unofficially my job to prevent, yet once it got to this stage I was helpless before it. At a certain point you could no longer separate Peter from his blood, from his body. To unpeel Peter from Peter, sometimes it just couldn't be done.

Francis, of course, didn't care about Peter's distress, and as I feared, he continued on, making explicit some things that should have remained forever in the past. "When you offered her up, did she have a choice?" *Offered her up* was a particularly unfair expression for what happened. Essentially, the truth is that Mao and Su Chen had briefly had an affair during the time she was an amah to Mao's two boys. This was something that I knew, though nobody had ever told me, in the ways of adults toward children. But in almost every historical account of Mao's life, and of the Cultural Revolution, there is a reference to a fight between Mao and his wife Jiang Qing about an amah, a babysitter. There must have been a thousand arguments of its kind, since Mao slept with so many women (and some men), but this particular fight was one that sent Jiang Qing and her entourage streaming into the countryside and up into Russia, where she vacationed at the Moscow spas. She was angry for months. If you put the dates together—May 1972 until March 1973—it becomes clear that it was Su Chen who was their amah, during most of that time.

It is well known that Mao's bed was enormous; he lived

inside the gates of Tiananmen Square and slept in the Hall of Chrysanthemums, banked with windows on one side, which opened onto a private garden. The rest of the walls were lined with shelves of books. His bed was emperor-size, which is three times king-size. Allegedly half of it was always covered with books, mostly the annals of the dynasties, all the terrible trespasses made through the years by the emperors. And the mistress, or the concubine, would recline on the bed and, if she was literate, read while she waited for Mao to appear. The carpet was apple green, apparently, and the room smelled of the jasmine and the gardenia that grew outside its garden doors. Mao, despite swimming laps every day, had gone a little soft. Sometimes I imagine what it must have been like for Su Chen, waiting in that beautiful room, that peaceful, learned room, the fronds outside the window waving, the flames flickering from the torches, as Mao came toward her. He was an enormous man really; he had a very large frame. He'd endured the Long March, in which for nights on end he'd slept in ditches and pulled lice from his body the whole night long, and ate only bowls of rice. He was a genius of revolution and a powerful man, and he was said to mesmerize women. If a person asks if Su Chen accepted him willingly or unwillingly, it's a near impossible distinction to make. This is the song every child sang before bed in those days, as did I: *The east is red; the sun shines; China has brought forth a Mao Tse-tung.* What if the person you sang about every night as you slipped into dreams was now striding toward you? The world, maybe even Peter, may well have disappeared for Su Chen in those moments. Who can say? When Chairman Mao inclines toward you, he blocks out the whole world. There would be just his frame, and the fire leaping at its edges.

I felt like shouting at them both that I had also loved Su Chen. I was tired of Peter forgetting that I had been there also. I had been under her *care*. Su Chen had loved me. She had spoken to me constantly under her breath. "Do not be a reed wavering at pond's edge," she had told me. "Your head holds up the heavens." I thought of her all the time, in her snowy grave, so far north that the snow never melts and covers without end the enemies of the state, all of whom carry on, if Confucius is to be believed, in the afterlife just as they had on this earth—ebullient, revolutionary, still brave even where bravery is no longer required but still cherished as a remnant of life on earth.

I believe that all of this meant as much to me as to either of them, for all of their stupid bravado and fear. I wanted to throw a drink in Peter's face to make it understood, but instead I led him out of the room and onto the rainy, blooming balcony (*Asia's in the heart!*), where the two of us recovered.

43

I walked down Broadway, ducked into Love's Discount to buy a new pair of tights for myself and some wine gums for Bram, and then headed across to Lafayette, where I caught a cab heading uptown. I was surprised by how happy I was merely because James was back in town. He'd been able to shoot all the scenes of his movie, or enough anyway to call it a wrap, against anybody's expectations, and we were celebrating today with Bram in paradise, which in New York City is Central Park. All the way up the island the crowds were without end until the cab turned onto East Eighty-eighth, which was as shady and serene as always, the craggy arms of trees reaching over the street, huge black birds gripping their branches like shadowy, shivering buds, and the architecture of the brownstones humble and beautiful in the gathering evening darkness. I made my way through the little courtyard in front of Lester Hotel, which brought to mind Peter's essay on courtyards and lobbies, places according to him designated as between here and there, "waystations where the umbrella is collapsed, the city shaken from the sleeve," he wrote, "and the person imagines what's to come beyond the oaken door." I had typed up that essay for him and had tried to gently question the word *oaken* as pretentious but he had insisted on keeping it.

I found James and Bramichari sitting in the library, at the far end in front of the fireplace. The smell of the fire was so evocative—nature burning away in the city—that I fell down eagerly into a big, overstuffed armchair, waving silently at both of them. James smiled, and Bram made the sort of deliberate, phony smile his mother had long ago taught him, which was very poignant to me. His mother had been at great pains, apparently, to give Bram lessons in what feelings *felt* like. And to a certain extent, it seemed that the lesson had taken hold. He had a somewhat formal, but very real and precise emotional life. The emotion that I discerned most powerfully in him was loyalty for his family and for their farm up in Saskatchewan. He didn't do any work on it exactly; he wasn't suited for really productive work, but it was Bram who walked those fields every morning and every night, checking the fences, giving its perimeter the full weight of his concern. In fact, when I would see the movie finally, nine months from this day, it would seem to me that the shots of the land were seen so austerely and distantly that they amounted to James's understanding of *Bram's* way of seeing, through eyes that were almost totally cleared of the seer's personality, both more limited and more free for this.

When we decided to go back into the cold, I lent my big cloak to Bram. He looked serious, like a count, when I lifted the hood over his head. We had decided to take a carriage ride. After a taxi dropped us off along the frilly southern edge of the park, we selected a gorgeous carriage, with a real cab that had an actual gold roof, all pulled by a white stallion. Bonnie-Beth always booed the carriages whenever she and I got near them, as she thought each carriage heavy enough to require at least two horses. So I looked around guiltily as I stepped up and in.

The day was getting colder, and the sun bluer, more icy. Everything seemed suddenly to shift back a hundred years or more as the cars disappeared behind us and the carriages took over, stately and orderly, their drivers in top hats, their riders covered in blankets. And as we were coming up and over the hills along Fifth, the last carousel ride of the day spinning to our left, the distant clinking of the zoo closing its great gates, the pastoral extravagance of the pond rolling away at our wheels, it also happened that somewhere deep in Manhattan the *Times* was printing off over a million copies of the next day's paper—December 4, 1993—which included on page 7 a tiny article outlining that Aquinas was being investigated for what they called "financial misdemeanors."

You could say the inside of that cab, for me, was essentially the room before the pain, the last place before things became for a time very sad. That's the place I'd go back to in my mind, again and again—the ivory handles on the doors, the tassels hanging from the seat in front of us, the torn black and shiny leather seats, the tiny doors with their half windows, and beyond the windows the city rushing by—green and gray, brilliant and blurry. And above us there was that little ceiling, embossed with scenes of the forest.

And yet, from inside the room before the pain, everything is always very clear, even crystalline—the rushing trees, the great city passing by, the *clop clop clop* of the horse's hooves. Taken on its own, each moment is fine, is just right, in spite of everything. Bramichari beside me had such private thoughts it was impossible to pursue them. With him one was free of the lugubriousness of emotions and relationships, free to look out at the trees and the city.

The horse and carriage took us up the hilly, winding street that roughly parallels Fifth Avenue and we wound along Central Park, a park whose sole purpose might just be to provide a natural place from which everybody can gaze back at the city, the buildings reflected in the reservoir like natural wonders themselves, their façades interpreted by the shivering leaves and long, strong arms of oaks. When we came up and over Seventy-second, we saw some of the large gray boulders that sit in the park, some as huge as the carriage itself, sitting there in the grass on the side of the road.

"Those rocks came down from Canada," Bram said. "During the Ice Age." There were some rivers of quartz running through the rocks, which were kind of lovely in a blocky, undisturbed way. They were hunkered down like huge hibernating animals, staring out across Fifth, toward the granite that unlike them had taken on an architecture and been organized into something useful, cut with windows, filled with glamorous rooms into which had been invited humans, all of which had also made the buildings vulnerable to time and the elements in a way that the boulders were not. It was unclear if the sacrifice was worth it or not, and the stones themselves appeared to be contemplating this as they faced out toward Manhattan rising in waves upon waves of complexity. "I'd like to go home now," Bramichari said.

"Okay," James said.

Our horse paused at a cross street to let some people by. There was a soft roar from the park life around us—crickets and birds and tree frogs mostly—and the trees that lined our road northward were a dark and active green. The night as it descended was taking on an almost human face, meaning it seemed to wonder how things would work out for all of us.

A Dicky-Dee bell rang twice and then three times, and the horse lit out again, northward—Bram, James, and I snug inside. I thought to myself that if the horse carried on, past the upper rim of the park, into Harlem and then out of the city, along the darkening shores of the Hudson, we would all eventually reach Canada, now already covered with a deep winter snow, and if we listed west a little the land would plateau back into Saskatchewan, those vast, snowy, and glowing fields, all of which is the journey the mind makes ceaselessly, tracing always the route home again.

Acknowledgments

I'd like to thank my parents, Don Lee and Marilyn Lee, for a life full of books, and love, and happiness. Also, thanks to my sister, Wendy Lee Arnold, who first introduced me to Asia, and for that matter to everything good. Thanks to my brother, Eric Lee, who has inspired and supported me. And for the most outrageous, fun times I have to thank my nephew Joshua Arnold and my niece Jessica Arnold. As well, many thanks to Steve Arnold for his generosity.

Thanks to the wonderful Beke family—Dr. John Beke, Beth Beke, Allison Beke, Paul Beke, and Kate Bilson.

Profound thanks to Stephen Beke and to Emma Beke, light of my life.

I'd like to thank my friends and many teachers along the way: Wendy Brenner(!), Leslie Bienen, Dana Sachs, Todd Berliner, Sarah Messer, Michael White, Karen Bender, Robert Siegel, David Gessner, Nina de Gramont, Phil Furia, Philip Gerard, Mark Cox, Dave Monahan, Tim Bass, Lavonne Adams, Brian Feltovich, Helen Dombrock, Clyde Edgerton, Kristina Edgerton, C. Michael Curtis, Dawn Lammer, Vanessa

Thorson, Leanne Stricker, Trevor Stalwick, Tara Wohlberg, Brita Lind, Michael Parker, Kathy Pories, Scott Thompson, Megan Hubbard, Carl Cherland, Malena Morling, Eric Vrooman, Laura Misco, Alan Wise, Beau Bishop, Hannah Abrams, Lorrie Moore, Jesse Lee Kercheval, Benjamin Anastas, Max Garland, Lee Schweninger, Tom Kunz, Gloria Mehlmann, Steve Polansky, Jeanette Kuiper, the late Mark Winkler, Frank Conroy, Ethan Canin, Bonnie Gordon, Verlyn Klinkenborg, Wayne Kallio, Margot Livesey, and the other Don Lee.

As well I'd like to thank the Radcliffe Institute at Harvard, the Rona Jaffe Foundation, the Creative Writing Department at the University of Wisconsin-Madison, the Iowa Writers' Workshop, and the Saskatchewan Writers Guild.

There are many books I leaned on during the writing of this book, most notably *The Timeless Way of Building* by Christopher Alexander, and Leslie Bienen's unpublished novel *The Star of Africa*.

This book would not have been published without the efforts of my brilliant, fast-acting agent, Doug Stewart, or without the ministrations of my editor, Denise Roy, who took over this book at exactly the right moment and found the story hidden inside.